BART HARDIN KNEW WHO THE KILLER WAS, ALL RIGHT—THE TOUGH PART WAS PINNING IT ON HIM.

The man who chilled the victim in the museum had a shatter-proof alibi, provided by none other than Bart Hardin himself!

The giant clue was a messy, daubed picture of a big, gaudy butterfly, painted by the stupid brother of Joe "The Whistler" Merusi—one of the toughest mobsters on Broadway.

Then "The Whistler's" brother turned up dead!

Broadway's feuds and murders move into New York's Museum of Modern Art in Dave Alexander's startlingly original THE MURDER OF WHISTLER'S BROTHER.

"FAST, SPIRITED, ATTENTION-RIVETING—ALEXANDER'S MOST SUSPENSEFUL TO DATE!"

New York Times

Books by David Alexander

the murder of, whistler's brother

A BART HARDIN MYSTERY NOVEL

BY

DAVID ALEXANDER

WILDSIDE PRESS

The Murder of Whistler's Brother

Published by Wildside Press LLC
www.wildsidepress.com

To JAMES ALBERT MILLER

of the Louisville *Courier Journal*
Gentleman, Scholar, Judge of Good Whisky—
and a Damned Good Newspaperman

Fly away, butterfly, back to Japan,
Tempt not a pinch at the hand of a man,
   And strive not to sting ere you die away.
So pert and so painted, so proud and so pretty,
To brush the bright down from your wings were a pity—
   Fly away, butterfly, fly away!

              —SWINBURNE: *To James McNeill Whistler*

one

Judge Millard Tevis had the gaunt, grim face of one of El Greco's painted saints, and he was greatly feared by lawyers, who had found him to be as stern and uncompromising as his bone-ribbed visage suggested.

He was presiding at the trial of The People Against Joseph Merusi for the murder of Jason Breck, which was in progress in Part IX of General Sessions in New York's Central Criminal Court. As court was called to order, the judge held a pair of black-rimmed glasses to his eyes and peered briefly at some notes in front of him. Then he lowered the reading glasses and turned his bleak gaze toward the defense table.

"Counselor," he said in the precise, parched, monotonic voice that had condemned countless felons to death or imprisonment, "yesterday the court granted your plea that this trial be recessed to permit you time to investigate new evidence and produce new witnesses. Is the defense now ready to proceed?"

The defense counsel, Marty Land, a slim, elegant man who bore the inelegant nickname of The Broadway Mouth, rose, bowed courteously, stood for a moment to allow the jury and spectators to admire his new and impeccably tailored suit. He said, "If it please the court, the defense is ready."

In the press row hard-bitten court reporters exchanged significant glances. Marty was wearing a flower in his buttonhole today. Land, a veteran of more than twenty years of legal battles in which a human life was often the stake, had many little mannerisms that were familiar. When he fingered his carefully waxed mustache, it was a signal that he was about to set off some unexpected fireworks. When he wore a flower in his buttonhole, it was almost always a token that he was about to fire a loud, resounding cannon. Marty had never lost a client to the electric chair, but it had been generally agreed

1

up to this point of the trial that only a miracle could save
the bookmaker, Merusi, who was known on Broadway as Joe
the Whistler because of his peculiar habit of whistling tunelessly through his teeth. Merusi sat beside his counsel now
and his clamped teeth and tightened facial muscles indicated
to those who knew him well that he was whistling, although
the slight hissing sound was so very soft only the persons directly next to him could hear it. He was a youngish man,
bulky and well dressed, and he was handsome in a dark-
browed, swarthy, Mediterranean way. There was no expression whatsoever on his heavily defined Latin features. There
hadn't been since the opening of the trial. He had refused
to offer any alibi for the time of the murder of Jason Breck,
even to his own lawyer. He had sat placidly through the hours
of police grilling before the trial. Now that the prosecution
was beginning to present the damning evidence against him
to the jury, he still sat placidly, unemotional and uncom-
municative, whistling softly and tunelessly. He had infuriated
his own attorney, the usually bland and imperturbable Marty
Land, almost as much as he had infuriated Lieutenant Romano of Manhattan West, the police officer in charge of the
homicide investigation.

The courtroom was packed. Jason Breck, the murdered
man, had been famous in the world of Broadway. He had
been a Ziegfeld of the night club business whose lavish pro-
ductions at the cabaret he called the Flower Garden on West
Fifty-sixth Street were one of the city's principal tourist
attractions. He had been a lone wolf, one of the very few
night club owners who had refused to take the Syndicate into
partnership or to knuckle down to the mob's racket-ridden
"unions." The Syndicate had good reason to want Jason
Breck dead, and Joseph Merusi, who handled the organization's gambling interests on the plush East Side of midtown
Manhattan, was a lieutenant of the Syndicate's hierarchy.
Also, Joe the Whistler had an urgent personal motive for
killing Breck. The prosecution had established beyond reasonable doubt that Joe had been having an affair with
Breck's young wife, Stephanie, a former Hollywood actress.

Behind the defense table, four men were sitting, all of
them seeming tense and strained, like fledgling actors waiting
in the wings for their cues to go onstage. The first of the men
was tall and lean and his hair was so extremely blond that it
seemed almost snowy, even though he was obviously still in
his thirties. In contrast to the hair, his face was surprisingly

dark, with a queer copperish tint. His features were strong without being either handsome or homely. His nose looked as if it had been broken once. It made a slight curve at the bridge that relieved the hard and angular pattern of bone structure. He was dressed conservatively except for a startlingly floral fancy vest. His name was Bart Hardin and he was managing editor of a sports and theatrical paper called the *Broadway Times*.

The man beside Hardin was Lucky Lou Krenech, a manager of prizefighters. He was a round and wheezy and very nervous little man who wore a chocolate-colored gabardine suit. He chewed at nails that were already bitten to the bloody quick. Next came a deceptively respectable-looking gray-haired man who wore a dark suit and rimless eyeglasses. Ralph Sleeth was a hotel manager, an honest enough occupation except that the hotel he managed was located in the Forties near Ninth Avenue and appealed mainly to patrons who paid in advance because they carried no baggage. Reputedly, the Syndicate owned and operated the hotel. The fourth man was thin, dark and razor-featured and wore sharp-cut Broadway tailoring. His name was Clint Merritt and he was the front for a Broadway theatre-ticket brokerage that was also supposedly owned by the Syndicate.

Judge Tevis looked toward the prosecution table. Before he could ask the question, the assistant district attorney trying the case, a red-haired, freckled young man named Amory Saltus, rose and bowed to indicate his readiness to proceed. The judge turned again to the defense counsel, who was still standing.

"I believe you were about to cross-examine the State's witness, Isadore Feldheim, at the time you moved for recess, counselor," he said. "Do you wish the witness recalled?"

Marty Land seemed to hesitate a moment, to debate the matter with himself. Then he said, "I should like to inquire briefly, Your Honor."

Isadore Feldheim was called to the witness stand. He was a small, shabby man of indeterminate middle age with a grizzled face and shifty eyes. He wore a rumpled tweed suit and a faded red sweater. He had already been sworn.

Marty Land took his time. He looked the witness over from head to foot and his attitude was one of studied insolence and contempt.

Finally the defense lawyer said, "I believe you testified under questioning of the District Attorney on Tuesday to the following facts, Mr. Feldheim. Please correct me if my memory is at fault. You stated that you are a cab driver. You stated that you are acquainted with the defendant, Joseph Merusi. You stated that you picked him up in your cab on the morning of September eighth, the morning that Jason Breck was murdered, in front of Dolly Buffo's Grill on Madison Avenue at two-thirty o'clock. You testified you drove Merusi to the home of Jason Breck on West Fifty-sixth Street, adjacent to his night club called The Flower Garden. Am I correct so far, Mr. Feldheim?"

The witness nodded his head vigorously. "Correct. Absolutely correct," he answered.

"Thank you. You stated that the defendant instructed you to wait outside the house for him and that you followed his orders. You stated you waited with the meter running for about half an hour, until three o'clock. You testified that you looked at your watch and that Merusi came out of the house at three o'clock exactly. Is that correct?"

"That's what I said," the witness agreed.

"You realize your testimony places the defendant in the home of Jason Breck during the crucial half-hour that the prosecution contends Jason Breck was shot and killed?" asked Land sternly.

The witness shrugged. "I can't help that. I swore to tell the truth."

"And you are telling the truth now, Mr. Feldheim?"

Feldheim glared angrily at the lawyer. "The truth and nothing but the truth," he answered stoutly.

"Now I believe you also testified that you then drove the defendant to his apartment house on Park Avenue and that he gave you a sum of money to forget this whole incident and that you thought nothing of it at the time because you had heard gossip to the effect that the defendant was having an affair with Mrs. Breck. Is that also correct, Mr. Feldheim?"

The witness was again nodding emphatically. "That's right. That's what I testified to the other day and that's exactly what happened."

"Thank you, Mr. Feldheim," said Marty Land. "Now I put it to you, sir. Do you wish to correct or retract all or any part of the testimony you have given in this court?"

The witness bridled. "Why should I?" he asked angrily. "It's the truth, every word of it. The truth, the whole truth and nothing but the truth. . . ."

Marty's words came so fast they almost interrupted the witness.

"That's all!" he barked angrily. He turned his elegantly tailored and eloquently contemptuous back to the witness and walked rapidly to the defense table.

Isadore Feldheim half-rose from the witness chair, then he sat down again uncertainly. Saltus, the prosecutor, had half-risen from his chair, too. His mouth was hanging open and his eyes followed Marty Land suspiciously. It was incredible. Land was the most ruthless cross-examiner he had ever encountered. Feldheim was the State's star witness, the witness who could seal the doom of Marty's client. Yet the defense counsel had done no more than make him repeat the damaging evidence he had already given under direct examination, had impressed that testimony even more vividly upon the jurors' minds. It was sudden, unexpected gambits like this that made Marty Land the most dangerous antagonist in the country. Young Saltus had been to court with Land twice before and had lost both times. He wanted to beat Marty Land far more than he wanted to convict Joseph Merusi. He wondered what Broderick, the D.A., the old Gray Fox himself, would do in a situation like this, what counter-move he might make. Land was apparently handing him the case on a silver platter, and that, of course, was just too good to be true. There was always more than an arm up Marty's well-turned sleeve. Judge Tevis was looking at Saltus inquiringly. So was the witness. The red-haired prosecutor rose from his half-sitting position and faced the grim, robed figure on the bench. He pondered a moment more and bit his lips. His freckled face was flushed rosily. Finally he said in a voice that was unduly loud to cover his confusion, "Your Honor, the State has no re-direct for this witness." He sat down.

"The witness may step down," Judge Tevis said, his shrewd, implacable old eyes on Land, who had again risen. From long experience, the judge knew that a thunderbolt was in the making.

Land addressed the court. "Your Honor," he said, "if the court please, the defense would like to put in several witnesses at this point. I know this is irregular. I assure the court that the introduction of such witnesses at this stage will expedite this trial immeasurably. Their testimony will clarify much of the evidence that has already been heard, both for the jury and for the court. I assure the court that their testimony will bear directly upon the statements made by the last witness."

Judge Tevis looked toward Saltus, expecting an objection. Saltus was so preoccupied he did not even see the judge. The expression on Tevis' pale, ascetic face did not change, but he was grinning inwardly. The young assistant D.A. was really sweating it now. He was conferring in whispers with Isadore Feldheim. Feldheim kept shaking his head in emphatic negation. Feldheim looked at the four men ranged behind the defense table and shrugged his shoulders elaborately. The jury and even the spectators noticed the gesture and interpreted it correctly. It said plainly, "I know nothing about them." When Saltus finally realized the judge was waiting for some expression from him, he, too, merely shrugged his shoulders, held his hands up, wide apart. He was telling the court, *I am mystified. It's up to you.*

Tevis said to Marty Land, "The prime object of a murder trial is not expedition, counselor. However, I am inclined to go along with you a little way, at least, to determine where the path may lead us. I warn you that any testimony you introduce must bear directly and immediately upon the evidence the last witness has given to this court."

"Directly, Your Honor," Land replied.

"You may call your witness," Judge Tevis ruled.

"I call Bart Hardin," Marty Land said in a loud, clear voice.

Hardin was uncomfortably conscious of the dead silence in the courtroom, of the scores of eyes that were fastened upon him as he walked toward the witness stand. He buttoned his dark jacket over the floral vest and wished that for once he had omitted the fancy garment that he affected half-ironically as an identification badge on Broadway, where mores demanded blatant advertisement of individuality. He did not like what he was about to do. He was glad enough to help Marty Land, who was lawyer for his paper, the *Broadway Times,* and a good friend besides. But he had no admiration at all for the defendant, Joe the Whistler, and rather suspected he might well have committed murder. Furthermore, he *had* admired Jason Breck, the murdered man, because he had been a tough-minded, rugged individualist who had had the guts to thwart the mob that ruled and owned most of Broadway's enterprises.

But there was nothing else that he could do, Hardin told himself.

After Hardin was sworn, Marty Land said, "Your name is Bart Hardin?"

Hardin agreed.

"Will you tell us your occupation, Mr. Hardin?"

Bart said, "I'm managing editor of the *Broadway Times.*"

"And the *Broadway Times* is a paper dealing mainly with theatrical and sporting news and it is published in the Times Square area of New York City, is that right?"

"That's right," Bart said.

"Now, Mr. Hardin, in your capacity as editor of such a paper, would it be correct to say that you meet and know a great many people in all walks of life in the world of Broadway? Would that be a fair statement, sir?"

Hardin nodded and said, "That would be correct."

Marty smiled blandishingly. The reporters in the press row noted with amusement that one of Marty's hands was fingering his mustache and the other was fingering the flower in his buttonhole. This was going to be a double-barreled explosion, apparently.

"Now, Mr. Hardin, I ask you to take your mind back to the early morning hours of September eighth, last, to the night that Jason Breck was murdered. Can you tell us where you were and what you were doing? Specifically, where you were and what you were doing and anything that may have occurred between the hours of two and three o'clock A.M. of that date."

Hardin said, "I was sitting in a poker game in a room of the Mid-City Hotel on Forty-first Street near Ninth Avenue."

"Thank you. And would you tell us approximately how far this hotel where you were playing cards is from the residence of the late Jason Breck on West Fifty-sixth Street near Fifth Avenue?"

Hardin's fingers were wriggling as he counted off the blocks. "Roughly, nineteen city blocks," he replied.

"Now, Mr. Hardin, were there others in this card game, this game of poker?"

"Yes, sir. There were four of us. Ralph Sleeth, the day manager of the hotel was playing. So were Lucky Lou Krenech, a fight manager, and Clint Merritt, a ticket broker. The game had been arranged by Moe Selig. He was supposed to play, but he never showed up. So we played four-handed all evening."

Land's face was a study in dewy innocence. "Who is Moe Selig, Mr. Hardin?" he inquired sweetly.

There was laughter in the courtroom. Even the jurors were smiling. Everyone in New York knew Moe Selig was a Syndicate boss, perhaps the right-hand man of Lenny Fassio, the overlord of all the rackets. And everyone knew, too, that Marty Land was Moe Selig's personal attorney. The judge rapped for order.

Hardin said, "I know Moe Selig as a gambler. I don't know what profession he lists on his income tax."

Saltus was on his feet, his freckled face flushed and furious. "I object, Your Honor!" he said loudly. "This is a travesty. This testimony doesn't bear . . ."

Marty interrupted, turning toward the bench with an expression as guileless and starry-eyed as that of a Boy Scout about to receive a Merit Badge. "Oh, it will bear, Your Honor!" he declared fervently. "I assure my worthy young opponent it will bear!"

Judge Tevis hesitated only a moment, his cold, keen eyes scrutinizing the defense counsel. "Objection overruled," he said. "You may proceed with your questioning, counselor."

"Thank you," Marty said disarmingly and turned back to Hardin. "Now, Mr. Hardin, will you tell us in your own words what occurred at approximately two-thirty o'clock on the morning of September eighth, last, in this room of the Mid-City Hotel where you and the others were playing cards?"

Hardin said, "We had agreed to break up the game at two-thirty. Mr. Sleeth, the hotel manager, said he had to get up early. Krenech had an appointment the next morning to look over some fighter. At two-thirty we stopped playing for a moment and debated whether we should continue for another half-hour. It was just at this time, not more than seconds later, anyway, that there was a knock on the door."

"And that was at two-thirty, or at latest, say, two-thirty-one on the morning of September eighth, last?" asked Land.

"Yes, sir. Sleeth, I think it was, got up and opened the door."

"And there was someone there?"

"Yes, sir. There was a Broadway cab driver I knew quite well. I knew him only by his nickname. His nickname was Busy Izzy."

"Do you see this cab driver, this man you knew as 'Busy Izzy,' in this courtroom, Mr. Hardin?"

"Yes, sir."

"Will you point him out, please?"

Hardin pointed to Isadore Feldheim. "The man who came to the door that morning was the witness who just testified," Hardin said flatly.

"You are quite certain, Mr. Hardin? You cannot be mistaken?"

"I am not mistaken," Hardin answered.

"And this was at two-thirty or two-thirty-one o'clock on the morning of September eighth, the exact time that Isadore Feldheim has testified that he was picking up the defendant in his cab in front of Dolly Buffo's Grill, some nine blocks from the Mid-City Hotel?"

"Yes, sir."

"Go on, please, Mr. Hardin. Did Feldheim explain his presence?"

Bart said, "He told us he had agreed to meet Moe Selig there. He said Selig's car was in the garage being repaired and he was to pick Selig up in his cab and drive him to his home in the suburbs."

"Did Feldheim leave immediately when he discovered Selig wasn't there?"

Hardin shook his head. "No, sir. We decided to double the limit and play for another half-hour. Feldheim stayed there the whole time. He said he'd promised Selig and he'd stay around in case he showed up. He remained in the room until the game broke up. The game broke up at exactly three-twelve o'clock."

"Then if Feldheim was in this room of this hotel from two-thirty until three-twelve he could hardly have been waiting in his cab in front of a house on Fifty-sixth Street, some nineteen blocks away, between two-thirty and three o'clock, could he, Mr. Hardin?"

Hardin merely shrugged his answer to that rhetorical question.

Land said, "Mr. Hardin, you did not come forward with the testimony you have just given until night before last, Tuesday night, when you visited me at my home, is that correct?"

Hardin answered in the affirmative.

"Now this murder occurred on September eighth, more than two months ago. Joseph Merusi was arrested and charged a few days later. The papers have been full of hints that the prosecution's star witness would be Isadore Feldheim, a cab driver, who had damaging evidence to offer against the accused. You are a newspaperman yourself and you must read the papers. Why did you not come forward earlier, Mr. Hardin?"

Hardin said, "In the first place I had no idea what Isadore Feldheim might testify. And I also had no idea that Isadore Feldheim was Busy Izzy, the man I knew. On Broadway you know many people only by their nicknames. That's the way I knew Feldheim. I did not discover that Isadore Feldheim and Busy Izzy were one and the same until Tuesday evening, when I came to you. I discovered it in this way. This case has a Broadway angle, because Jason Breck was a night club owner and was married to a Hollywood actress. Also, the defendant is well known on Broadway. I sent my photographer, Pete Cruise, down here. He took a picture of Isadore Feldheim. That night he threw the print on my desk and said, 'Guess who the star witness is? Our little friend, Busy Izzy!' I recognized him then, I remembered his presence at the card game and I realized the testimony he had given could not be right. So I came to your house."

"Thank you, Mr. Hardin. And to make this clear to the jury, I asked for a recess at the opening of court on Wednesday in order to subpoena the necessary witnesses. Now, Mr. Hardin, just once more: Isadore Feldheim came to this room where you were playing cards at what time on the morning of September eighth?"

"At two-thirty or a few seconds later."

"And he left at what time?"

"When the game broke up. At three-twelve exactly."

Land stood in front of Hardin for a moment silently. He kept casting sly, sidelong glances at Saltus. There was another question to be asked, of course. The jury expected him to ask it. The judge obviously expected him to ask it. Even the spectators seemed to anticipate it. But the answer would come so much more devastatingly if he could trick the prosecution into asking it instead. If Broderick, the old Gray Fox, had been trying the case, Land would never have dared to leave it hanging. Broderick was wary. He did not walk into traps. But the freckled Saltus was young and he was an eager beaver. He seemed to be champing at the bit now, waiting his turn to tear into Hardin. Saltus, Land decided, would take the bait. A little smile flickered beneath Marty's trim, bristling mustache. He was going to throw young Saltus to the lions.

He smiled warmly at Hardin, said, "Thank you, Mr. Hardin. I have no more questions." He turned to Saltus and bowed politely. "Your witness, Mr. District Attorney," he said.

Saltus was on his feet before Land was seated. He charged

to the attack the way a young bull might lunge at a fallen picador.

"Mr. Hardin, do you keep a diary?" Saltus asked.

"No," Hardin answered.

"Mr. Hardin," said Saltus, his tone of voice soft and coaxing, "will you agree with me that it is very difficult for anyone to remember exactly what he did on a certain day two months ago unless it was a birthday or a holiday or some special occasion?"

"Sometimes," Hardin answered cagily.

"And will you agree with me further that it is even more difficult, if not impossible, for the average person to remember at what exact minute of some date two months ago a casual and seemingly unimportant incident occurred? Will you agree to that, Mr. Hardin?"

"Usually," Hardin fenced.

"Yet, Mr. Hardin, you remember not only the day but *the exact minute* that a taxi driver walked into a certain room and you remember to *the exact minute* how long he remained there on a date two months ago, even though your acquaintance with this taxi driver was so slight that you knew him only by his nickname. Now you don't really mean to swear to a thing like that before this court, do you, Mr. Hardin?"

Marty Land grinned widely. He winked affably at one of the grizzled veterans in the press row. Saltus had taken the bait. He had swallowed it whole. Saltus was as dead as a mackerel in a fish store.

Hardin said calmly, "I have sworn to it, and I believe others will swear to it, and it is a fact. The time of Feldheim's arrival was fixed in my mind by the fact that we had agreed to end the game at two-thirty and that Sleeth and I were both wearing watches and we were comparing them at the time the knock came at the door. It was two-thirty and our watches agreed to the second. The time that the game broke up and the exact date on which it was held are even more firmly fixed in my mind, probably because I like to gamble and gamblers often follow hunches. I won a pot and Sleeth looked at his watch and said, 'It's time to quit. It's twelve minutes after three.' I looked at my own watch and it was three-twelve exactly. Isadore Feldheim was still there in the room at the time and he had not left the room. I remember saying, 'Three-one-two is a good number to play in the numbers bank tomorrow.' I had played the numbers game for years and never won once. The odds against you are enormous as the payoff is five hundred to one. I played two dollars on three-one-two on September eighth, and the number came up. I won a thousand dollars and a gambler doesn't forget the day he won a thousand dollars for a two-buck investment too easily. When I identified Feldheim's picture, however, I checked to make sure. The winning number is derived from the various totals of pari-mutuel betting at the racetracks. The *Broadway Times* runs these mutuel totals for the benefit of numbers players. I checked our files and three-one-two came up on September eighth. It had not come up before in many months, possibly in many years, if ever."

During Bart's long recital, the assistant D.A.'s red, freckled face had gone ashen. Marty Land observed the young lawyer, an amused twinkle in his eyes. The poor boy's good as dead, he thought. I may as well bury him decently. He rose and addressed the court.

"Your Honor," he said humbly, "I'm afraid the defense must plead to a serious oversight." He held up a newspaper. "I have here the September eighth issue of the *Broadway Times* in which is printed the pari-mutuel totals in question from which the number three-one-two is derived. I was remiss in not placing it in evidence and I apologize to the court."

Old Judge Tevis' face crinkled for a second. It might have been a bitter smile. Oversight, he thought. He held it out on purpose, of course, the tricky devil. He was smart enough to make the prosecution do his dirty work and shatter their case completely by doing it.

Judge Tevis had the newspaper marked for exhibit and placed in evidence, but even as he did so he thought it was a rather futile formality.

It took the young District Attorney some time to recover from a condition that closely resembled a state of shock. He never did come out of it completely, but he roused himself enough to go through the motions. He tried to discredit the witness because Hardin liked to gamble and because he admittedly played the numbers bank, which is illegal. He tried to belittle Hardin's standing as a newspaper editor because the *Broadway Times* dealt with the world of amusements and sports, but he was not successful. The *Broadway Times* was one of the oldest papers in New York City and it was well known to the judge, the jurors and everyone in the courtroom. Saltus failed completely to shake Hardin's testimony and when Bart finally stepped down from the stand, the assistant

D.A. knew that Marty Land had beaten him again. Without the testimony of Feldheim, his case collapsed completely.

The three other witnesses, Sleeth, Krenech and Merritt, were put on the stand. With them Saltus was slightly more successful. Their standing was rather dubious. All of them had had brushes with the law, all of them were skittish and evasive and none of them would have made a good impression on judge or jury under ordinary circumstances, since it was all too obvious that they lived on the shady side of Broadway and had Syndicate connections. But they corroborated all of the essential points of Hardin's testimony and Saltus was unable to make them back down.

When Merritt, the last witness, stepped down, Marty Land rose and addressed the court.

"If the court please, the defense has a motion," he said.

"You may make your motion," the judge said shortly. Saltus half-rose again, seeming to feel he should oppose a motion that had not yet been made, but it took only a withering glance from Tevis to silence him and make him collapse disconsolately into his chair.

"The defense moves for dismissal of the case of The People Against Joseph Merusi on the grounds that the only testimony the State has produced to place the defendant on the scene at the time of the murder of Jason Breck has been proved to be perjured," said Marty Land, his fingers caressing the flower in his buttonhole in the way a winning horseplayer might fondle a good-luck charm.

Judge Tevis said immediately, before the assistant district attorney could even rise, "The court is going to grant your motion, counselor. Before it does, however, there are certain remarks the court has to make."

The old judge glared at the perjured witness, who sat blank-faced in a chair near Saltus. "I instruct a court attendant to take in charge the witness known as Isadore Feldheim and place him in custody to be held for a possible perjury indictment before the grand jury of this county," said the judge.

A uniformed court attendant moved to Feldheim's side at once, as if he had been anticipating the judge's order.

Tevis turned to the jurors. "I feel the court owes the good citizens who have discharged their civic duty by serving on this jury an apology," the old man went on, his voice a kind of relentless drone. "It is sad and it is reprehensible that the State has come to this court with unclean hands and it is my intention to demand the most searching investigation into the conduct of this case by both the District Attorney's office that placed Isadore Feldheim on the stand and the police officers who caused the arrest of Joseph Merusi."

Now Tevis was staring straight at Saltus and Saltus was sweating profusely. "I do not charge that the District Attorney's office was criminally culpable in this matter to the extent that it had foreknowledge of the witness' perjury," he declared. "I do charge that it was criminally culpable in presenting this witness without a far more thorough inquiry into his credibility, and, in so doing, making a travesty of the majesty of the law."

The judge's eyes were searching the big courtroom. Finally they found what they were seeking and his gaze settled on a beefy, dark-faced man in the back of the room who was mopping his face with a handkerchief. The man was Lieutenant Romano, of Homicide, Manhattan West, who had been in charge of the police investigation of Breck's murder. "I intend to consult with the police commissioner regarding the police responsibility in this matter and the methods employed by the officer in charge of the investigation," Tevis declared.

Hardin winced. The officer in charge of the investigation was Romano, and Romano, who was sometimes called the only honest cop on Broadway, had been Bart's friend for many years. Romano was not far from retirement and, in the politics of the police department, this thing could hurt him seriously.

The judge had turned his attention to Hardin and the other three defense witnesses now. "Finally, I express the profound appreciation of this court to the witnesses who have come forward voluntarily to set right a gross and incredible legal blunder that might well have cost a man his life."

The judge picked up his gavel and rapped once. "The case of The People Against Joseph Merusi is dismissed," he said in the same frigid voice with which he sentenced defendants to the electric chair. Judge Tevis rose and walked rapidly from the court, his robes billowing behind him like visible black clouds of his anger.

Joe the Whistler would walk out of court a free man. He had been placed in jeopardy and he could never again be tried for the murder of Jason Breck.

The court attendant moved off with the unprotesting Feldheim, clutching his prisoner by the arm. Reporters clustered about Marty Land and Joe the Whistler. Bart Hardin walked rapidly from the courtroom. He looked over his shoulder and saw that Joe the Whistler was trying to push his way out of the welter around him. Joe was trying to signal to him, but Bart paid no attention. He did not want Joe the Whistler's thanks for what he had just done.

It was bright noon of a cold November day when Hardin walked out into Centre Street.

He wondered if he had been the instrument of setting a murderer free.

two

Like many other residents of midtown New York, Bart Hardin found this downtown section with its maze of State and Federal and municipal buildings, walled in by the granite cliffs of the financial district, a trackless jungle. He stood helplessly on the curbing, flagging cab after cab, only to find that each was occupied. He stood there for ten minutes or more and he became so desperate he even contemplated taking a subway, a thing he did in only the direst of emergencies. He was about to move off in search of a subway station when he heard a suave, familiar voice behind him.

"Really, boys, I couldn't tell you whether he's the sixty-third or sixty-fourth client I've managed to keep out of the death house without consulting my records," Marty Land was saying to a group of reporters. "Why don't you ask old Jim Beach of the *World-Telegram?* He's got a mind like an IBM machine."

One of the reporters said, "You ought to subsidize this guy Hardin, Marty. You were dead as a Kansas Sunday until he happened along. Maybe you could have established reasonable doubt to a jury by putting on those other jokers, but you'd have never got a dismissal. Old Tevis wouldn't believe 'em if they told him today is Thursday."

"Speaking of my good angel," said Marty, "here he is, frantically seeking transportation, apparently." He put his hand on Hardin's shoulder. "I wondered where you'd got to. You disappeared like the lady in the magician's cabinet. Can I offer you a ride uptown? That's a very small subsidy, I admit."

"You can," said Bart. "Apparently all the cabs down here come equipped with passengers."

"Hey, Hardin!" called a tabloid reporter Bart knew slightly.

16

"You gonna get a piece of the Whistler's book? It's the second biggest one in town."

It was nothing more than a good-natured gag, of course, but for a moment Hardin was furiously angry. Marty seemed to sense Bart's tenseness. He led him quickly to a parking lot for court officials around the corner and they got into Land's big, hearse-like Cadillac.

"You'll have to trust yourself to my driving today, I'm afraid," Landis said. "My houseman and my chauffeur both take Thursday off. I've always wondered why household employees insist on taking Thursday off. Did you ever hear of anything important or amusing happening on a Thursday?"

Marty lived his busy and pleasant bachelor life in an elegant little private house on East Sixtieth Street. He was barely fifty and he shared with Los Angeles' Jerry Giesler the distinction of being the nation's most famous trial lawyer.

When they were in the car and headed north, Marty said, "If I forgot to say thanks— Well, thanks. I was going to lose this one without you. Even poor Saltus couldn't have bungled enough to blow this one for the State. I've got a kind of childish pride in my unblemished record in murder cases, too. I've copped a few pleas, of course, but up to now, none of my boys has burned."

Marty tapped a hardwood accessory that was one of the fittings in the elaborate car as he made the boast.

The attorney looked sidelong at Hardin, who only nodded abstractedly. "Something's bugging you, boy," he said. "I can tell. What is it? You've done a good deed. You've saved a man who's obviously innocent from death. Does that bug you? Why?"

"Are you sure he's innocent?" Bart asked.

"No," said Marty, "I'm not. The fact is, I just don't know, any more than you do. What we both do know is the fact that he would have been convicted on the evidence of a perjurer if you hadn't come along."

Bart said, "It's going to go hard with Romano."

"That part I don't like," Land admitted. "Romano is a good cop and a decent man. I like him tremendously and I always have, despite his constant complaints about his imaginary ailments and despite the fact that we are always on opposite sides when the battle lines are drawn.

"Still, he's been on the force for nearly thirty years. He should know how to roll with the punches. I can't understand him consenting to base a whole case upon the testimony of so dubious a character as your friend and mine, Busy Izzy. Busy Izzy has been a police stool pigeon before, of course, but he has always been scrupulous about not offending the underworld combine. In fact, Izzy has always been an errand boy for the Syndicate, which owns the cab company for which he drives."

Land gave Hardin a sidelong glance as he continued, "The miscreants he has informed against in the past have invariably either been felons outside the combine who proved a nuisance to the Syndicate or they have been backsliding employees who required disciplining. The Syndicate has a habit that is most annoying to the District Attorney's office. It often uses the law to achieve its own intents and purposes."

Marty turned the wheel sharply and steered away from a trailer truck that was crowding him.

"I simply can't believe that Joe the Whistler was in trouble with the boys and that they planted their stooge to testify against him," Marty declared. "The Whistler is said to be a pet and protégé of Lenny Fassio himself and he is a close associate of Moe Selig. His book is enormously profitable to the organization. The Whistler's ingratiating manners seem to appeal to the upper crust and he has a carriage trade from Madison and Park and Sutton Place, while Moe Selig handles the professional gamblers of Broadway. Why, under such circumstances, Izzy should dare to bear false witness against a high-echelon member of the mob that has been his benefactor poses a pretty problem.

"He had nothing to gain and a great deal to lose, including his life. It may well have been a personal grudge, of course. The perjury indictment may be a godsend for our Izzy. Prison should insure him temporarily against reprisal."

Bart was still thinking of Romano. He said, "About the only way I can see that Romano could square this beef would be to produce new evidence to prove the Whistler was guilty. But that wouldn't do any good, anyway, would it, even though it was a dismissal and not a jury verdict?"

Marty shook his head. "My client can never be tried again for the murder of Jason Breck," he declared. "To do so would be to place him in double jeopardy. There is a slightly hazy area of legal precedent so far as dismissals are concerned as to just exactly when a defendant is placed in jeopardy, but one principle has been thoroughly established by the appellate courts. Once a prosecution witness steps to the stand to testify against a man, that man is in jeopardy and can never be tried again for the same offense."

"The more I think about it, the surer I am that the Whistler got away with murder," Bart said bitterly. "And that I helped him. The Syndicate wanted Breck's night club because it was the biggest one in town, and they couldn't get it because Breck was one man on Broadway who wouldn't play ball with goons. The Whistler belonged to the Syndicate and he wanted Breck's wife, only he couldn't get her because she wouldn't give up all that nice, soft money.

"By killing Breck he could get the night club for the Syndicate and Mrs. Breck for himself. To me, it adds, except that Busy Izzy was lying in his teeth. I liked old Breck. I admired his guts. You knew him, didn't you?"

Marty nodded. "I knew him well. A big bony man who always reminded me of Abe Lincoln without a beard. He was something of an anachronism on modern Broadway with that wardrobe of black and baggy clothes that the late McKinley might have worn to his Inauguration. He was a strong man, but women were his Achilles' heel. His taste for beautiful women made him a fortune in the night club business, but he had a regrettable habit of taking wives half his age who eventually left him, taking large hunks of alimony with them."

"Women were about his only weakness, though," Bart declared. "He was a tough old man. He had the guts to tell the mob to go to hell and he got away with it for years and his Flower Garden was a decent place with good entertainment and not a sucker trap. It makes me feel kind of dirty when I think I may have helped the man who murdered him."

"Stop bugging yourself!" said Marty sharply. "You did the only thing a decent man could do. You knew a slimy little stoolie was lying and that his lies were about to send a human being to the electric chair. Stick to that. Maybe you don't like the Whistler. Maybe I don't either. But all we know against him for sure is that he runs a book and played around with an old man's young wife. That isn't sufficient grounds for me to refuse to defend him or for you to refuse to testify in his behalf when your testimony brought out nothing but the truth."

As Marty steered the car toward Broadway, he said, "I'll tell you something. In many ways this was the damnedest case they ever threw in my lap. Until you came along like the cavalry in the silent movies, I had just one screwy and flimsy fact to rely upon. Whoever murdered Jason Breck took paste replicas of Mrs. Breck's jewelry from the apartment. She collected antique jewelry, you know. All the pieces were authenticated as having belonged to historic personages like the Empress Josephine or Madame Pompadour. The real goods were in a safe-deposit vault, of course. But the fact that the paste replicas were missing might persuade a jury that a thief rather than a jealous lover or a Syndicate triggerman had killed Breck."

Land stopped for a traffic light and fidgeted a moment. As the light turned green he continued, "It wasn't much to work with. And the main thing that made me think the Whistler was probably innocent was his flat refusal to offer the police or even me any kind of alibi. He simply said he couldn't remember where he was on the night of the murder. That wasn't in character. When a mobster murders he usually has a whole room full of witnesses to swear he was some place other than the murder scene at the time. They aren't very credible witnesses as a rule, but at least they may serve the purpose of casting reasonable doubt on the issue. Joe had none. I would have expected Selig to produce a few in the Whistler's behalf, since Joe had been negligent about doing so. But he didn't. There wasn't a peep out of Selig the whole time. Nobody came forward to help the Whistler in his time of need. And he refused to try to help himself. Think that over, and maybe you won't feel so guilty."

Bart got out of the car at Forty-ninth and Broadway. It was only a few blocks from the *Broadway Times* office and he wanted to stop in Selig's horse room and bet on a horse he liked in the third at Narragansett.

Before he drove off, Marty said, "Quit brooding. It makes wrinkles. You did the right thing. It was the only thing you could do. Tell you what. My household staff's off today and I'm eating out. Meet me at seven-thirty at the Saddle and Whip Restaurant and I'll buy you a steak that's big enough to milk."

Bart nodded glumly. "All right," he said. "I always eat there, anyway. If I've loosed a murderer on the town I may as well get a free meal out of it."

Marty grinned and roared off in the big Cadillac. Bart turned west on the strip of Forty-ninth Street between Broadway and Madison Square Garden that is fondly known as "Jacobs Beach" in memory of the promoter who retained an iron-fisted stranglehold on the prizefight business for the greater part of his lifetime. The beach is bordered on both sides by drab hotels, ticket agencies, bars and brownstone residences with scaly façades. On one side is a Catholic church and across from it is a smoke shop that has never sold a cigarette, cigar or ounce of pipe tobacco. It is the front for Moe Selig's headquarters. Behind the smoke shop is the biggest horse room in New York.

At this noon hour the Beach was crowded as usual with late-rising citizens of the Big Street. Their eyes, still sleep-gummed, scanned racehorse past performances and scratch sheets. In front of a hotel a little group of expostulative fight managers was gathered, cursing the Boxing Commission.

Marty Land had a heavy foot on the throttle and a fine disdain for traffic laws. It had not taken long to drive uptown. But the age-old grapevine is the speediest system of communication man has ever invented. News that Joe the Whistler had beaten the rap had preceded Bart to Jacobs Beach. That was obvious almost immediately. The Broadway beach-combers ordinarily approached Hardin with a half-apologetic hat-in-hand respect that had always faintly amused him.

Hardin edited a paper that deal with racing, boxing, theatre and night club news, the principal interests of Jacobs Beach citizens, yet the paper pulled no punches. It was the consensus on the Beach that you couldn't buy Hardin and that it was a good idea to stay in his good graces.

Today, however, the attitude of the hangers-on toward him was oddly different. Several men with whom he had a mere nodding acquaintance approached him familiarly and even patronizingly as he walked toward the horse room to make his bet on the third at Narragansett. A slim character known as Paddock Sam Purvis, who served as one of Selig's layoff men at the tracks, sidled up, his wide grin revealing tobacco-rusted teeth.

Purvis' greeting to Hardin usually consisted of a quick, salute-like flick of a finger to his wide hatbrim and a hurriedly mumbled, "Hiya, Mr. Hardin?" Today he slapped Hardin's back, said loudly, "Hiya, kid! I hear you sprung the Whistler. You ought to get three points the best of the odds from Selig any time you ask!"

The anger Bart had felt when the tabloid reporter hailed him on Centre Street returned. He didn't trust himself to answer Purvis. He merely brushed him off and walked on toward the horse room. But there were others. Pearly Bowes, a fight manager who often came to the *Broadway Times*, wheedling and begging for publicity for one of his palookas, stuck out a pudgy paw decorated with a flawed diamond and cried heartily, "Congratulations, Bart! They tell me you hit that D.A. with an uppercut that jarred his eyeballs. They tell me if it hadn't been for you the Whistler would have burned for sure. I hear that Lou Krenech sweat off twenty pounds when they had him on the stand and couldn't talk above a whisper he was so nervous. It was you who did it, Bart! Everybody says so."

It was the first time Pearly Bowes had ever addressed Hardin as "Bart." Hardin had to shake off several other well-wishers before he got to the smoke-shop entrance of the horse room.

There was a prop counter containing prop displays in the smoke shop and behind the counter was an old man with a mastiff face who might have been a tobacco salesman. He wasn't. His name was Eddie O'Grady and he was a hero of World War I and an inveterate gambler. On Broadway he was known as the Old Top Sarge. The Sarge was employed as a lookout for Selig's book. It was a convenient arrangement both for O'Grady and for Selig. The Sarge's small living expenses were paid by a government pension. He lost his salary back to Selig every week in the form of horse bets. Bart had known the old man for years and was fond of him. He often staked him and employed him for odd jobs.

The Sarge beamed at Bart as he entered the shop. "Hello, there, Captain!" he said in a booming voice. "I heard all about it! Moe Selig will be mighty glad to see you today, I bet. I guess you can have about anything you want around this joint from now on in!"

Bart realized the Sarge meant well and was honestly happy over his good fortune of being in right with the mob. The old man had had one great day of glory on the Western Front back in 1918 and had won the Congressional Medal of Honor. Ever since, he had existed in this half-world of Broadway gamblers and he accepted its code without question, even though he had never been a part of its viciousness. The Old Sarge's mind never carried him far beyond the last race for today or the first race for tomorrow. The stupid implications of the old man's remark stung Bart, even though he realized the offense was unintentional.

Hardin said, "Come to think of it, I don't want anything, though." He turned and walked rapidly to the street without going into the back room to make his bet on the horse at Narragansett.

As he walked toward the *Broadway Times* office at Eighth Avenue and Fifty-first Street, he thought bitterly, *So now I'm one of the boys. Bart Hardin, the Syndicate stooge.*

The *Broadway Times* had been doing business for more than fifty years in an ancient building that had been a nine-teenth-century firehouse. As Hardin entered, Bertha, the switchboard operator, greeted him enthusiastically. "Hello there, Mr. Hardin!" she exclaimed. "Why, you're real famous, I hear. They had your name on the city news wire, all about how you saved that bookmaker from the electric chair."

"Sure," said Hardin bitterly. "Maybe some day I'll be as famous as Lenny Fassio and Al Capone."

As he strode rapidly across the enormous city room to the beaver-boarded cubicle that served as the managing editor's office, he was followed by curious glances from the men who were pounding typewriters, reading copy and drinking coffee from cardboard containers.

Old Jim Lennox, Hardin's "secretary," was waiting for Bart in the office. He was a small man with an almost angelic innocence written on his face, and he was well into his seventies. He had had a long and distinguished career as an actor on Broadway and then had known years of grim poverty. Bart paid the old man out of his own salary to per-form small and generally pointless functions. He said it was worth the money just to look at an honest man on Broadway. Jim had acquired a feather duster somewhere and was making fussy little gestures with it, attempting to brush away the dust and grit that coated the desk and filing cabinets and virtually everything else in the old building.

Lennox's face lighted up as Bart came in. "Good morning, Bart!" he said happily. "I heard about the judge's ruling. It must be a wonderful feeling to know you've saved a human life."

"I'm not so sure that it is in this case, Jim," Bart said. He hung up his coat and hat and seated himself at a rolltop desk which seemed as old as the *Broadway Times.*

Presently old Pops Taylor, the turf editor, rose from the slot of the horseshoe copy desk that circled around the brass pole fire laddies had once used as an emergency exit and ambled toward Hardin's office. Pops, who had worked on the paper for forty years or more, had little respect for

managing editors, although he was fond of Hardin. He peered
over his half-moon glasses at Bart, who was sitting in a swivel
chair beside the battered rolltop desk.

"Hear you kept the Whistler from getting his tail scorched,"
Pops said. "First damn time I ever heard of a horseplayer
going out of his way to help a bookmaker. Personally, I think
all bookies who keep the twenty-to-one limit on should burn."
Old Pops was a compulsive gambler and a longshot punter.
"You bet that goat I tipped you on in the third at Narragansett?" he asked. "He's eight to one and your money back
in the morning line. The track's turned soft up there, too.
He'll breeze."

"I went in to bet on him, but I changed my mind," Bart told
the old man.

Pops shook his head. "Never change your mind," he advised. "They always win when you change your mind."

He ambled out again.

Hardin tried to lose himself in work, but his mind was
only partly occupied with the day-book and layouts and proofs
and copy piled in front of him.

He had a vague, uncomfortable feeling that somehow he
had been framed into doing the thing that he had done,
yet there could be no possible doubt that he had told the
exact truth about the perjured witness, Busy Izzy. The thing
simply made no sense, though. Why had Izzy, who eked out
his precarious existence on the fringes of the mob, suddenly
turned from a mouse into a roaring lion who had the brazen
courage to sit on a witness stand and lie against one of the
mob's most important bosses? The obvious conclusion was
that Fassio and Selig wanted to get rid of Joe the Whistler
and had used Busy Izzy for their purpose. Almost always,
though, when a mobster became "hot" rumbles were out on
Jacobs Beach and Bart heard them. Hardin had heard no such
rumbles about the Whistler. Joe had seemed as solidly en-
trenched as Selig or even Fassio himself.

Bart shook his head. I don't think they framed Joe the
Whistler, he told himself. I think they framed me. But I'm
damned if I can see how or why.

There was another puzzling angle to the whole business,
too. Selig had arranged the poker game in the Mid-City Hotel
on the night of the murder and Selig hadn't shown. But Izzy
had shown up, looking for Selig, at the exact time he was to
swear he was somewhere else. For nearly three-quarters of an
hour, Izzy had stood in full view of four men who could

swear he wasn't sitting in a cab that was parked in front of a house on Fifty-sixth Street where murder was being done. If Selig had been framing the Whistler, he would hardly have had his stooge do a thing like that.

The mid-afternoon editions of the papers did not improve Bart's state of mind. The horse at Narragansett he had failed to bet on because of a fit of petulance had won, at good odds. But even worse were the headlines:

JUDGE BLASTS D.A., POLICE OFFICER
IN DISMISSING MURDER CHARGE

All of the stories implied plainly enough that while there had been four witnesses for the defense, it was Hardin's testimony that had clinched the dismissal since the editor had been regarded as a more reputable and trustworthy citizen than the others who had played in the card game on September eighth.

Bart picked up the phone and tried to call Romano at Manhattan West. He wasn't quite sure what he would say to the lieutenant, except to tell him rather foolishly that he was sorry for his part in this unpleasant business. A desk man informed Hardin that the lieutenant was out.

Hardin hardly led a disciplined life, but he was at least a creature of habit. It was his custom to take a break every day at four o'clock and walk to the Sligo Slasher's Bar on Forty-ninth for his first drink of Irish whisky. Today he remained in his office and took a drink from the bottle in his bottom drawer. He excused this interruption of routine by the fact that he had arrived at the office late because of the trial and work was piled up in front of him. He knew this was not the real reason. At the Slasher's he would almost certainly encounter Broadway idlers who would want to make talk about the trial and about his own prominent part in it. Usually, Hardin did not meet a situation by running away and hiding. He was doing that now, though, and he had to admit it to himself.

It was after seven when he finally put the paper to bed and marked the ink-stained first-run copies for correction. He walked to Broadway to keep his engagement with Marty Land at the Saddle and Whip.

The Saddle and Whip was the only fine restaurant on Broadway that hadn't been crowded out by orange drink stands, penny arcades and souvenir shops. It was an old place that dated back to the days of Diamond Jim Brady and the Floradora Sextette and it was very expensive. The fight managers, bookies' runners and errand boys of Jacobs Beach did not congregate here. Only the upper-echelon mobsters could afford the prices. Several of the Syndicate's captains were present as Bart entered, along with theatre people, newspaper columnists and prosperous tourists. A few of the Syndicate bosses greeted Bart. He sensed at once that their attitude toward him was subtly different from that of the flunkies who had accosted him that morning. The underlings had indicated plainly enough that they believed Hardin had sold out to the mob. The Big Boys prided themselves on possessing a sense of humor. Many of them even carried court jesters around with them to serve as the butt of crude and sometimes cruel practical jokes. The mob bosses in the Saddle and Whip appeared to regard Hardin with humorous condescension, as if he had been the unwitting victim of one of their more elaborate and side-splitting pranks. Bart decided he liked this attitude even less than that which he had encountered earlier on Jacobs Beach.

Hayden of the Saddle and Whip was famed as the biggest headwaiter on Broadway. He stood over six feet tall and weighed in the neighborhood of three hundred pounds. He approached Bart now with that subtle mixture of deference and intimacy that is an attribute of all good maîtres. "Mr. Land has already arrived, Mr. Hardin," he said. "He's waiting for you in the alcove."

The alcove contained a big round table that would accommodate six, fenced off slightly from the main dining room. "Is it a party?" Bart asked, surprised.

"No, sir. Just dinner for two. But when Mr. Land asks for the alcove, Mr. Land gets the alcove," Hayden answered.

As Bart approached, Marty rose and stuck out his hand. He had a dry martini in front of him and an Irish on the rocks was waiting for Bart.

When Bart had seated himself, Marty said, "We're going to have a visitor a little later, it seems. He called up and wanted to know where I'd be, so he could deliver a present to me. He also has a present for you, I understand."

Bart's eyes narrowed. "Who?" he asked suspiciously.

"Benny Merusi, the Whistler's younger brother. You know him, don't you? One of the few good things I know about my client, Joe the Whistler, is his devotion to his kid brother.

Benny fell from the fire escape of a slum tenement when he was a child and injured his head. He's mentally retarded, of course, but he is completely harmless and in many ways he is entirely lovable. He was in some county institution for a while, a place for mentally defective children. They taught him fingerpainting as therapy. They seem to do this now with the mentally ill as well as with kindergarten pupils. Benny became completely fascinated with fingerpainting, and oddly enough he's achieved some rather amazing effects among his copious works. He must have produced literally hundreds of fingerpaintings. I have been the recipient of dozens myself. Whenever Benny likes you, he gives you a fingerpainting as a token of his affection."

Bart nodded and smiled. "I know," he said. "He took a liking for me, too, a while back and he's showered me with samples of his work. I've got one of his pictures tacked to my office wall, along with photographs of night club cuties and racehorses. Benny told me it was his impression of a horse in motion."

Marty grinned. "I suppose we're going to be presented with further Merusi masterpieces as an expression of Benny's gratitude for our part in helping his brother out of what might be termed euphemistically an embarrassing situation," he said. "Benny is now employed by the Museum of Modern Art. He's there through my auspices, in fact. I was recently made a director of the museum, you know. He works nights on the maintenance crew. Actually, he's a kind of janitor who sweeps the floor, but he doesn't think of himself as that. He thinks of himself as a watchman who guards all those beautiful paintings. He seems very happy and I understand he is a trustworthy employee. Benny has been fascinated by bright-colored pictures ever since he learned the art of fingerpainting. He used to haunt the museums, and I thought it might help the poor boy to adjust if he had a job in one of them."

Bart said, "If Benny gives me many more paintings, I'll have to build an annex to my flat. His work is now piled in a corner beneath a stack of soiled laundry."

"Benny's prolific output even strains the storage space in my house," Marty replied. "But it would break his heart if I refused one of his offerings. He did a rather interesting thing once in tones of black and gray. I had it framed and hung it in my office. Maybe you don't know that the real title of the famous painting popularly known as 'Whistler's Mother' is

'Arrangement in Gray and Black, No. 1.' I call the Merusi abstraction in my office 'Portrait of Whistler's Mother by Whistler's Brother.' "

Marty and Bart were to have an unexpected guest before Benny's arrival. They had just finished their shrimp cocktails and were waiting for the steaks when Lieutenant Romano was ushered to the alcove.

three

Romano's appearance shocked Hardin. The lieutenant's face, usually swarthy, had a sick, gray look to it and it was drawn by lines of strain. His chunky body had always seemed solid to Bart. Suddenly, it appeared flabby. But there was something else about Romano that impressed Hardin, immediately the detective began to speak. There was a new, hard, unrelenting quality to the man, as if he were motivated by some inner, driving force that bordered on the fanatical.

Romano nodded to Marty Land, said, "I don't like interrupting your dinner but there's some things I want to tell you and I heard I'd find you here." He turned toward Bart, said, "Hello, Hardin. I'm glad you're here to listen to what I've got to say."

"By all means. Sit down, Lieutenant, and have some dinner with us," Marty said cordially.

Romano shook his head. "No. I just had a bowl of soup. My nervous stomach is acting up. I couldn't take a heavy meal."

"A drink, then," Marty suggested, starting to signal for the waiter, but Romano stopped him.

"Booze is no good for the stomach," he declared. "All I want is just to tell you something. First, I wasn't too happy about going to court with nothing but motive and the testimony of that Feldheim. I've known Busy Izzy a long time. I wouldn't trust him with a red-hot stove. I wanted to wait and dig up more before we went to court. But Izzy told about as straight a story as I ever heard and Broderick, the D.A., who doesn't know him as well as I do, wouldn't wait. You couldn't blame him too much. He's been trying to convict one of the top ones in the organization a long time now

29

and he's never been able to catch one with his pants down like this before. He figured Joe the Whistler was about the third ranking man in the combine, right next to Fassio and Selig. So he wanted to get to court before something had happened to his only witness, while he could still keep him on ice. Maybe he let his enthusiasm get the best of his judgment, I don't know. But if ever a man acted guilty, the Whistler did. He didn't even try to give us a fake alibi. He acted like a whipped cur. But I wanted to tell you that I didn't know Busy Izzy was lying to us. There didn't seem to be any possible reason for him to lie. And the D.A. didn't know it, either."

Marty said, "I never suspected for a minute that either you or Broderick knew, Lieutenant. I have to put on an act in the courtroom. I charge big retainers and my clients expect that much. But I knew you and the D.A. had been sold a bill of goods. I was sure of that."

Romano nodded his head. "Thanks," he said. "I've got something else to tell you. Your client's guilty as hell. He killed Jason Breck. He killed him just as sure as I've got gas pains in my nervous stomach. I'm going to get Joe the Whistler."

Both Bart and Marty were regarding Romano with concern.

Marty said, "That doesn't sound like you, Lieutenant. It doesn't sound like you at all. You can't 'get' Joe Merusi for the Breck kill. Legally, that's impossible. He's been placed in jeopardy by the State itself."

"I'm going to get him just the same," Romano declared. "I just thought I'd warn you, put the cards out on the table. I've got nothing to lose. I've been in the Commissioner's office all afternoon getting my tail eaten off. I was getting right up to the top of the Captain's List and now I'm right down at the bottom, even if they don't force me to retire. I can't make the Whistler burn for chilling Breck. But I'm going to make Joe the Whistler the most miserable bastard on Broadway."

Marty shook his head. "You're overwrought, Lieutenant. You know that there are laws against the police persecuting a man who is legally innocent and you know me well enough to realize I'll invoke those laws."

Romano said, "I'm leveling with you, counselor. I can do it and I will. I've done it before. Maybe you don't remember Marletto. You weren't the top mouth on the Big Street in those days, back in the thirties. Slick Sam Saltzman was.

Things were tougher in those days, counselor, and Marletto was tougher than Joe the Whistler ever was. He was a cop-killer among other things. I brought him in when I was off duty and wasn't wearing any metal but the zipper on my pants. I had three witnesses that time, good witnesses, but Slick Sam Saltzman got to them and they changed their testimony. Marletto beat the rap. We hounded Marletto and we hounded everybody he spoke to. We made him so hot that the mob had to get rid of him. They dumped him in a vacant lot in Brooklyn one rainy night. You can tell your client I'm going to hound him the same way, Marty. That's what the score is going to be."

Marty drummed fingers on the table. He said, "Listen to me a minute. I knew Marletto and I know what happened. It wasn't the first time it had happened. But there was a difference. The defense had perjured witnesses in that one. In the Merusi case it was the prosecution that put a lying witness on the stand. The D.A. and the Commissioner are going to want to hush this one up as fast as possible. They aren't going to want to keep it alive by hounding the Whistler and getting public sympathy for him. With Marletto, you had the whole force working with you, because the police were right and they knew it. This time the police were wrong. If you do this thing, you'll do it alone and you'll even do it against orders and you'll do it purely for personal motives. That won't be good, Lieutenant. It won't be good for you, I mean."

"I'm going to get him just the same," Romano declared stubbornly. "Maybe if I can tie him up with this Breck murder so there can't be any doubt, even though we never can convict him, I'll be able to persuade the brass and I'll have the force to help me again, like I did with Marletto. If I've got to do it alone, I'll do it alone, even if it costs me my job and my pension. I thought I ought to tell you, Marty."

Marty shrugged helplessly. "I wish you wouldn't, Lieutenant. It's my job to protect my client and I do my job. I'd rather have you for a friend than an enemy, mainly because I like you. I honestly don't think you can hurt Joe the Whistler any. But I'll tell you one thing. If you persecute him, you can hurt yourself a lot."

Romano rose, said, "Thanks for telling me, counselor. Just let your client know Romano is out to get him. I wouldn't want to take him by surprise."

Bart started to speak. "Listen, Romano . . ." he said.

The lieutenant held up his hand. "Don't apologize to me for what you did today," he said, "and don't sympathize with me. I know you did what you had to do. That's the trouble with being a cop. People always do what they have to do. Sometimes that's kind of bad for cops."

He nodded a curt farewell and walked away from the alcove.

Marty's gaze followed Romano's broad back. After a moment he said, "When he came here he looked like a beaten man, but he didn't sound much like one. He's doing the wrong thing for himself. If he could persuade the high brass that I got Joe the Whistler off through legal trickery, he might hound my client right out of his dubious business with the help and co-operation of the whole department. But he can't persuade the Commissioner of that under the circumstances and he'll be doing it alone. It can mean the end of his career, and his career's been a pretty damned fine one up to now."

The waiter arrived with the steaks. Marty noted Bart's stricken face and tried to make a small diversion. "I hope you gave the chef my instructions, Andy," he said to the waiter.

The waiter grinned. "I told him just what you said, Mr. Land. I told him, Mr. Land wants the steaks really rare. I told him you said not to kill the steer, just to tap him lightly on the head and stun him."

Marty attempted to make desultory conversation through the rest of the meal, but Bart's face was sober and he answered only in monosyllables.

They were having coffee and cigars when Joe the Whistler's brother Benny arrived.

Benny was a plump, soft-looking youth, with a vacuous, good-natured expression on his broad face. His movements were hurried and impetuous like those of a excited child. He was carrying two flat, wrapped packages under his arm. Marty winked at Bart as Benny approached and whispered, "We are about to be presented with more original Merusis, I see."

Benny bumbled up to the table breathlessly and said, "Hello, Mr. Land and Mr. Hardin. I was scared I wouldn't catch you. They was taking down an exhibit of what they call American Primitives at the museum and I was a little late getting my coffee break."

Marty smiled amiably at the youth. He said, "Welcome,

Benny. Sit down and have your coffee with us. Was the exhibition of Primitives a success?"

He turned to Bart. "There was some controversy among the directors about having a museum of modern art exhibit the work of the untutored painters of the eighteenth and early nineteenth centuries, since most of it ranked as Americana more than art, anyway.

"The exhibit was centered around a small painting recently presented to the museum by one of our richest trustees, Carlton Wainwright. It was a newly discovered landscape by the most famous of the American Primitive artists, one Edward Hicks. Hicks was a sign-painter and itinerant evangelist who preached against the world's frivolities. He must be whirling in his grave if he knows the exorbitant prices his works are bringing today."

Benny seated himself tentatively on the edge of a chair without removing his coat. His eyes were round and wide like the eyes of a child in a toy shop. He said, "There was big crowds at the exhibit, all right. I heard somebody say it was the biggest success in years."

Marty laughed. "It's an amusing commentary on the citizens of the world's most sophisticated city that they should come in droves to gape at the nostalgic relics of our ingenuous past," he said. "I was among them. I would like very much to own the Hicks landscape, in fact."

Benny's eyes were bright and eager. He said, "Could I have a piece of pie with my coffee?"

Marty looked at the youth indulgently. "You're getting fat, Benny," he said. "Sweets are bad for you. But I suppose it's all right to celebrate your brother's deliverance."

"With green ice cream?" asked Benny. "My brother Joe brought me here for dinner on my birthday once and I had apple pie with green ice cream."

Marty called the waiter. "Apple pie à la mode with pistachio," he said.

Benny did not make his presentation of gifts to Bart and Marty until he had finished the slab of pie surmounted by the soft green hillock of ice cream. Finally he wiped his mouth and said to Marty, "I brought you and Mr. Hardin some presents to thank you for what you did for my brother Joe today."

He handed one of the flat packages to Bart and the other to Marty. He was smiling in happy anticipation. He said to

Bart, "Your present ain't quite as good as the one for Mr. Land, Mr. Hardin. It's just a fingerpainting that I did myself. But you liked my picture of the horse and this one is even better. It's the best one I ever did. Only there's something I got to tell you. When you open it up, just take a quick peep and don't let anybody see it.

"My brother Joe would be awful sore if he knew I gave it to you. When I told him about it, he said I had to give it to him so's he could burn it up, but I don't want him to burn it up because it's the prettiest picture I ever painted. Only you mustn't tell anybody, especially my brother Joe."

Marty said, "Why does Joe want you to burn it, Benny? I thought Joe liked your paintings."

Benny shook his head. "I don't know," he said. "Joe's got lots of my paintings. He's got some of them in frames, even. He says he's going to rent what they call a gallery sometime and have an exhibit of Benny Merusi fingerpaintings, but I think he's just kidding me. Anyway, he didn't even see this painting and he says he's going to burn it up. I just told him about it and he wanted me to give it to him right away, but I didn't want to, so I stalled him. You keep it in your house, Mr. Hardin, and don't let anybody see it, you understand?"

Bart opened the wrapping and looked at Benny's fingerpainting. So did Marty. Benny was glancing apprehensively over his shoulder, like a conspirator.

It was a painting of a butterfly. A very special butterfly, with a star-shape on its outspread wings. The over-all design was one of small, multi-colored circles in orderly patterns. The paint had the glowing quality of stained glass.

Bart said, "I agree with you, Benny. This is the best painting of yours I've seen. It kind of gleams."

"Cover it up quick," Benny said in an urgent whisper. "Here comes the waiter. I promised my brother Joe I wouldn't let anybody see it, but I knew I could trust you and Mr. Land."

Bart covered the painting. The waiter cleared away Benny's dishes and refilled the water glasses. When he left, Marty opened his own package. He stared at the painting for a moment in amazement. Bart regarded Marty curiously. Benny was fairly bursting with happiness.

"My God!" exclaimed Marty, speaking very softly. "This is the Hicks landscape that Wainwright presented to the museum! It can't be a copy. It's the original."

"That's right," declared Benny, a huge smile spreading over

his childish face. "You said you liked it, so I robbed it for you."

Marty covered the picture hastily. "Benny, don't you realize what you've done?" he asked. "This painting is worth a small fortune. Don't you know it's wrong to steal?"

Benny's face fell. "I guess you don't like it because I didn't bring the frame," he said. "I was afraid they'd notice if I brought the frame. I'm always carrying my own fingerpaintings in and out of the museum wrapped up in paper, so they wouldn't pay any attention to me walking out with a couple of packages. Sometimes I show my fingerpaintings to the other fellows when we're cleaning up at night and they stick them up on the wall like they was exhibits and they stand around like they was museum visitors and talk about them, just for laughs. But my pictures aren't framed. I took this one out of the frame before I robbed it so they wouldn't notice anything."

Marty shook his head. "Benny, it's not the frame," he said. "It's the fact that you stole this picture, can't you understand? Don't you know it's wrong to steal, Benny?"

"Why?" Benny demanded, tears of exasperation welling to his eyes. "You talk crazy, just like the man at the juvenile court they took me to when I was twelve years old because I robbed some neckties for my brother Joe. My brother Joe liked to dress up sharp when he went out with girls and he didn't have many clothes and we didn't have any money so one day I saw all these pretty neckties on a counter and I robbed some for him. There wasn't nothing wrong. Joe needed the ties. The store man didn't need them. He had plenty more."

Benny looked appealingly at Marty. A tear was sliding down his plump, pathetically foolish face. "Don't you see?" he asked. "They was going to put this picture back in a storeroom and keep it with the permanent collection and maybe they wouldn't bring it out and let anybody look at it again for a year or even longer. What's the good of that? You said you like the picture. So you can hang it up on your wall and look at it all the time. What's wrong with that? If you really want the frame, I'll try to rob that for you, too, but it won't be so easy."

Marty put his elbows on the table and squeezed his head between his hands. "Benny, Benny," he said despairingly. "Some day soon you and I are going to have to have a nice, long talk about right and wrong and the law and a thing called ethics. But there's hardly time for that now. You're in a bad jam solely because you tried to do a nice thing for me, and I want to get you out of it if I can." He touched Benny's arm. "It's not that I don't appreciate your kind thought, Benny," he said. "It's just something I don't seem able to make you understand. You could go to jail for this, or back to an institution. Now, listen to me. Listen to me carefully and do exactly what I say. Get back to the museum immediately and try to act as if nothing has happened. Don't mention to anyone that you saw me. Just do your work as usual. And under no circumstances admit that you know anything whatsoever about this painting. You understand?"

Benny rose. His face was heavy with grief and disappointment. "Okay," he said. "I'll do what you tell me, Mr. Land. I'm sorry you didn't like the picture. Maybe if I could've brought the frame you'd have liked it better."

He started off, then turned back and bent down to Hardin. "Don't say nothing about the butterfly," he whispered portentously.

As soon as Benny left, Marty called for the check. He said to Bart, "We've got to get out of here. I want you to come up to my place on Sixtieth. For the second time today, I need your services as a witness."

Marty hadn't brought his car. They flagged a cab on Broadway. Bart noted that Land gave the driver an address a couple of houses removed from his own residence, but he did not comment. Marty's ways were often devious when he was intent upon protecting a client's interests, and Benny Merusi had suddenly become a client, apparently. After Marty paid off the driver, he said to Bart, "I want you to wait here for about thirty seconds. Then come up to the house. I want you to be able to testify truthfully to something that's about to happen."

Bart was puzzled, but he followed Marty's orders. When he went to the house a few moments later he found Marty waiting for him at the bottom of the stoop. They mounted the steps. Marty looked down at a package that was propped against his front door. "Now I wonder what that could be?" he said. "It must have been a very inefficient delivery man to leave a parcel out here in the open like that."

Marty unlocked the door and they went into the quietly luxurious living room that had always seemed to Bart to be so alien to the brash public personality of the Broadway Mouth. Land opened the package and pretended amazement when he discovered the Hicks landscape inside. Hardin knew no actor on the Broadway stage who could have put on a more convincing performance. Marty consulted an address book and dialed the number of Carlton Wainwright's residence.

He said into the phone, "Carlton? This is Marty Land. The most amazing thing has just occurred. A friend of mine, Bart Hardin of the *Broadway Times*, and I dined out this evening. We came to my house a few minutes ago and we found a package propped against the door. It's my man's day off and I thought some careless delivery boy had left it there until I opened it. It's the Hicks landscape that you presented to the museum, Carlton! I can swear it's the original and not a copy!"

Land waited while the receiver resounded with a *bassoprofundo* buzzing. Then he said, "I'm sure I'm as much at sea as you are, Carlton. I can only guess that the thief failed to dispose of the painting and got cold feet. He must have known I was a director of the museum and left it here as a way of returning it to its rightful owners."

Marty listened patiently to the crackling receiver again. He said, "Of course it's upsetting, Carlton. But at least the painting doesn't appear to be harmed. Listen, neither you nor I live far from the museum. Why don't we meet there as soon as possible? I'll bring the painting and we can give it to the night custodian and see it's locked up safely pending an investigation. Fine. In half an hour, then."

Marty hung up the phone and sighed heavily. He said to Bart, "If anybody knows Benny was the workman supposed to store the Hicks landscape, he's in for trouble, but I doubt the hired help in a museum distinguishes between one picture and another any more than a bank clerk distinguishes between one dollar bill and another. Anyway, we've done the best we can for the poor boy."

Marty rewrapped the painting, since he was afraid the police might be able to trace the original paper to Benny somehow. He poured a drink for Bart. "We have a little time," he said. "I keep a bottle of Irish here against your too infrequent appearances." He poured brandy for himself and sat down in a leather chair.

"Sometimes," said Marty, "I'm inclined to wonder if children and mental defectives aren't the only truly rational people. Perhaps the blow to Benny's head years ago cleared his cerebellum of the usual rubbish that guides our lives and left only the important and logical motivations. His arguments

were a rather devastating confutation of our age-old legal
and ethical system, I'm afraid. Why, in all reason, should a
painting from which I derive great enjoyment be stored in
a temperature-controlled, locked room merely because of the
accident of ownership?"

Ten minutes later they left and found a cab. Bart did not
want to lug Benny's painting of the butterfly around. He left
it at Marty's house. Marty had the Hicks landscape clutched
tightly under his arm. He directed the driver to the Museum
of Modern Art on Fifty-third Street between Fifth and Sixth
avenues. As the cab approached the museum, Marty's brow
wrinkled. "That's odd," he said. "The place is blazing with
light. It closes at six and it's after ten now. Ah, I see our
friend Wainwright stalking about in front like an impatient
sentinel. He is a notoriously punctual man. He must be awaiting us anxiously."

Something else was awaiting them.

Something called murder.

four

Wainwright rushed up to Land as he emerged from the cab. "This is terrible, Land! Terrible!" he exclaimed. He was a big, aging, heavy-jowled man and his voice had a deep resonance that attracted the attention of a little knot of passersby who had been drawn by the police cars Bart now saw were parked near the entrance to the museum and by the uniformed policeman at the door.

"Take it easy, Carlton," Marty said soothingly. "It's not so bad. The painting's safe at least."

"The painting! I'm not talking about the painting, man! Why do you think these policeman are here?"

Marty said, "I assumed you must have called them, Carlton. Because of the stolen painting, of course."

"Not at all! They were here when I arrived a few minutes ago. There's been a murder in the museum, Land! Imagine that! A murder! In the museum!"

"Who?" asked Marty. "Who was murdered, Carlton?"

"I don't know his name. Some fellow on the night maintenance crew, I understand. Got hit over the head in the Sculpture Garden. Hit his head on the base of a statue when he fell. Split his head wide open, it seems! Terrible!"

Marty thrust the wrapped package into Wainwright's hands. "Take this, Carlton," he said. He walked rapidly toward the glass and chromium door of the museum. Bart was at his heels. The policeman barred their passage, but Lieutenant Romano emerged from the interior immediately and said, "Let them in. I want to talk to them."

Bart and Marty followed Romano into the lobby of the museum.

"Where's your client, counselor?" Romano said to Land.

"I have lots of clients, Lieutenant," Marty replied. "Which one are you seeking?"

39

"Your most recent client. Joe the Whistler."

"You're not trying to pin another murder on him already, are you, Lieutenant?" Marty asked.

"Not necessarily," Romano answered. "I just thought maybe he'd like to know his kid brother has been killed."

"Benny?" said Marty. "It seems impossible. He was with Hardin and me not more than an hour ago."

"Where?"

"In the Saddle and Whip Restaurant. He came there to give Hardin one of his fingerpaintings as a token of his appreciation for testifying for his brother."

"I know all about Benny and his fingerpaintings," Romano declared. "Benny was a good boy. It's too bad his brother Joe didn't fall on his head, too. It might have made him more like Benny." Romano turned to Hardin. "You got this painting he gave you?" he asked. "Not that it matters much, probably."

Bart shook his head. "I left it up at Marty's house," he said. "It couldn't mean anything. It was just a painting of a butterfly."

Romano's brow crinkled. "A butterfly," he said. "That's funny. Somehow or other it seems I ought to remember something about a butterfly, but I don't."

Carlton Wainwright bustled up. "What's this about a painting?" he asked. "I'm a trustee of this museum, sir. Did Mr. Land tell you about the stolen Hicks painting? Has that something to do with the murder? It was a rarity, sir, a real rarity. Only recently discovered. Hicks usually painted historical or Biblical scenes or animals, you know, but this was a landscape. A priceless discovery . . ."

"I bet it was," Romano interrupted him. "I bet it was real pretty, too. Okay, Land, what's he talking about?"

Land said, "Carlton, you're going to hate me, and I value your friendship. I lied to you. The fact is I didn't find the Hicks painting propped against my door. It was given to me tonight by the man who was murdered. I tried to protect him because he was mentally sick and did not have the average person's conception of right and wrong. Benny Merusi stole the painting from the museum. He gave it to me because he knew I admired it and he thought it was going to be put away so nobody could enjoy it. To him it seemed the right thing to do."

"I'm astonished, Land!" Wainwright exclaimed. "A director of the museum protecting an art thief! It's incredible!"

Romano said, "Okay, Marty. Benny stole a valuable painting from the museum and gave it to you. Where is it?"

"I have it right here," said Wainwright, unwrapping the package. "Mr. Land called me and arranged to meet me here to return it. He gave me some cock-and-bull story about finding it propped in front of his door."

Romano took the Primitive and looked at it. "So this is art," he said. "It looks like one of the pictures my daughter used to paint when she was a little girl in school."

"Well!" exclaimed the outraged Mr. Wainwright. "I didn't realize policemen were art critics, sir. Allow me to assure you that a landscape by Hicks is a rarity and its value is incalculable."

"Yeah," replied Romano. "Like I said, it's real pretty. You think somebody might have killed this Benny because he stole it? Maybe I'll have to hold it for evidence."

Wainwright bridled. "No!" he exclaimed. "I will protest to the District Attorney's office, sir! To the Commissioner! As a trustee of this museum I certainly do not intend to trust a valuable painting to the tender mercies of policemen!"

Wainwright's concern was solely for the painting, Bart thought. He seemed to have forgotten the corpse in the Sculpture Garden completely.

Romano hadn't. He handed the painting back to Wainwright, said, "You can keep it till I need it, anyway." He turned to Marty Land. "All right, counselor," he said. "I'm asking you again. Where's your client?"

Marty said, "Right there, Lieutenant." He motioned toward the big glass doors of the museum which had opened to admit a very young and immature-looking patrolman who had his hand clutched firmly on the arm of Joe the Whistler. Joe the Whistler was hatless and disheveled. His shirt was open at the throat, he wore no necktie and his thick dark hair was uncombed.

As the young patrolman came forward with his quarry, Romano said, "Where'd you find him?"

The Whistler was a powerful man. He shook off the young cop's grip angrily, said to Romano, "What's this about my brother Benny?"

Romano didn't even look at Joe. He said to the patrolman, "I asked you where you found him."

"In the Breck house on Fifty-sixth," the cop answered. "The house was almost dark and we had to ring the bell and pound on the door five minutes before they opened up.

This man came to the door half-dressed. He had on his pants and undershirt and he was in his bare feet."

"What about the woman, Mrs. Breck?" Romano answered. "Was she there? Did you bring her in?"

The young man's face flushed. "Yes, sir. She's out in the prowl car with McCarthy. She—she wasn't dressed. We had to wait till she put some clothes on." The officer's youthful face had turned bright red by the time he finished the sentence.

"I asked you what about my brother, copper," the Whistler said loudly. "This cop told me he got killed. Is that the truth? Where is he?"

Romano paid no attention whatsoever to the Whistler.

"How long did Merusi claim he'd been inside the house?" the lieutenant asked.

The policeman bit his lip and averted his eyes, embarrassed. "He . . . he said he'd been there ever since late this afternoon. Mrs. Breck came down dressed in a kind of robe and she said right out that they'd been there since this afternoon and that they didn't answer the door right away because they'd let the servants off and they were undressed and they were in a—a bedroom at the back of the house and didn't even hear us until we started breaking down the door." The young man was almost tongue-tied by embarrassment, but he forced himself to continue. "She said right out that they hadn't left the bedroom at all for several hours. She claimed they hadn't even eaten dinner!"

"I want to see my brother, copper!" the Whistler said furiously.

Romano turned to him as if he were conscious of his presence for the first time. He said, "Your brother's dead, Merusi. Somebody slugged him with a blunt instrument, probably a blackjack, not more than an hour ago. His head hit the base of one of those statues in the garden and it cracked wide open. You know, I remember something, Whistler. They brought you in once a few years back for carrying a concealed weapon. The weapon was a blackjack, if I remember right."

Marty Land said, "Easy now, Lieutenant. You have no basis whatsoever for such an imputation unless they found a weapon on Merusi's person this evening. The arresting officer seems to agree he has accounted adequately for the time of this murder and that he has a witness."

The young cop shook his head at Romano, said, "When we found him there wasn't anything on his person except his pants and undershirt. We didn't find a weapon in the house, but of course it hasn't been searched thoroughly yet."

"We'll search it thoroughly," Romano declared. "And we'll search his own apartment."

"Listen, copper, I said I want to see my brother," the Whistler repeated. "If somebody killed him and I find out who it was, there'll be no need for the law. I'll take care of it. My kid brother wasn't quite right in his head, maybe, but he never harmed anybody in all his life. He was a good kid, too damned good to be true almost. I'll take care of the one that killed him, copper. I don't need you."

Marty spoke sharply. "As your attorney I warn you against making rash statements, Joe," he said. "I realize, of course, and I'm sure the lieutenant realizes, you are speaking in the heat of emotion brought on by this shocking event."

Romano snorted contemptuously. "Come on," he said. "I'll show you your brother, Whistler. The medics and the ID men should be through with him by now. Bring your mouth along with you. Land knows what a lot of murderers look like. Maybe he'd like to take a gander at one of their victims."

Romano lifted a velvet rope at the entrance beside the admission desk, nodded toward the right, walked without haste to the rear of the museum. The Whistler followed him, with the young cop still close at his side. Marty followed his client. Bart hesitated for a moment, then joined the procession. No one tried to stop him. From the outside, the museum had seemed to be brilliantly lighted, largely because the lights immediately adjacent to the huge glass door had been turned on. The interior was shadowy. In a twilight corridor arabesque textile designs by Matisse glowed dully like the illuminations of ancient manuscripts.

Romano pushed a glass door and they followed him to the Sculpture Garden. The Sculpture Garden was a large patio planted with greens that were sere and small trees whose branches were naked and antlerish at this time of year. The area was flooded now by lights set high up in the masonry of the building. There was a small pool with flat marble bridges in the center of the garden and ranged around it were massive sculptures by Rodin and Epstein and Malliol and Lipschitz. The bronze and marble figures, many of them abstractions, threw weird, enormous shadows in the icy glare the floodlights cast on the courtyard stones.

On the near side of the pool Rodin's famous statue of

Balzac reared from a high pedestal. Around the base of the statue a little group of men was clustered, many of them kneeling like worshippers at a votive altar. Their movements and their voices came startlingly in this little world of still and silent figures.

The body of Benny Merusi lay on its back beneath the statue of Balzac in a small red pool of its own. Benny's broad, foolish face stared up and his eyes were wide and innocent and unbelieving. From across the way one of Lipschitz's nightmares in metal glared with huge and round and baleful eyes. Above Benny towered the cloaked Balzac, arrogantly posed and contemptuous of this Human Comedy at his feet.

The Whistler stood looking down at his brother. Bart was amazed to see that there were tears in his hard eyes. "There wasn't any use," he kept saying. "There wasn't any use in killing Benny. He never meant any harm to anybody."

The assistant medical examiner was rattling off the facts he had gleaned from his superficial examination. Benny had certainly died instantly and he had died within the hour. He had been knocked down by a hard blow to his temple from a blunt instrument and his head had been split open when it struck the sharp edge of the statue's base.

"Was it the blow from the blunt instrument that killed him or was he killed when his head struck the pedestal?" Marty Land asked eagerly.

"I don't think a p.m. will show that," the medical examiner said. "It could have been either one or both. He wouldn't have fallen if the blunt instrument hadn't struck him, though. And if he hadn't fallen, his head wouldn't have hit the pedestal."

Romano grinned unpleasantly at Land. "You trying to cop a plea already, counselor?" he inquired. "Let me tell you something, then. I'm going to try for Murder One on this if I can get the evidence. Not Murder Two. Not Manslaughter. Murder One, first degree, the kind of murder that puts their fannies down in the electric chair when a jury finds 'em guilty."

The lieutenant turned abruptly to the young cop. "Take Merusi down to Twentieth Street," he said. "I'm holding him for questioning." As an afterthought, he added, "Put the bracelets on him."

"Just a minute now, Lieutenant," Marty said quickly. "This man's brother has just been murdered. Merusi is obviously grief-stricken and in shock. There is no possible motive for him killing his brother. There is no logical reason to connect him with this crime. He has answered questions as to his whereabouts and a witness has confirmed his story at considerable personal embarrassment. You have no right and no reason to question him further. Certainly you have no right or no reason to take him down to Homicide in handcuffs. I'm speaking as his attorney, Lieutenant."

The young cop had the handcuffs out. He stood uncertainly for a moment, looking from the lawyer to Romano.

Romano said to the young policeman, "I'm taking him in. Put the handcuffs on him. And I'm taking in the woman, too."

Marty's voice was frigid now.

"I feel I should warn you, Lieutenant. You're making a mistake," he said. "This thing has become a personal vendetta with you. There may be some excuse for you questioning my client briefly because he is the brother of the murdered man. That does not justify your holding him at police headquarters. It does not justify your putting handcuffs on him. You failed to convict this man of another murder today because of the perjury of a police witness. That is rankling. There is no other possible explanation of this extraordinary procedure. You can't get away with using your police power for personal revenge, Lieutenant. I prefer to use the velvet glove, but I can be a very tough adversary when I have to be. If you do what you propose, Marty Land is getting tough."

"You threatening me, Marty?" Romano asked. He grinned at Land almost amiably.

Marty said, "I've known you a long time, Romano, and I like you. But Marty Land protects the interests of his clients, no matter who gets hurt."

Romano nodded, accepting it. "Don't just stand there," he told the uniformed policeman. "I said he's going down. And he's going down in bracelets."

The policeman put the handcuffs on Merusi. The Whistler started to protest, but he was silenced by a nod from his lawyer.

The other police officials, the harness bulls and the ID men and the medical examiner, were watching Romano curiously. It was all too plain that they doubted the wisdom of his action, that they thought he was being stubbornly foolish.

Marty said, "If you are taking my client in, I insist upon accompanying him."

Romano shook his head, "You aren't accompanying him

at city expense," he declared. "There's no room in the prowl cars for a hitch-hiker."

"In that case, I'll follow in a cab."

Romano shrugged. "Nothing illegal about that, so long as you pay your fare," he said.

"I'm going to wait at Manhattan West," Marty continued. "I'm going to wait for a reasonable length of time. After that I'm going to take action. I want you to know that, Lieutenant. I want you to know exactly what I'm going to do. If my client is held *incommunicado* for what I consider an unreasonable length of time, I will first call the District Attorney and make a personal protest over the continued persecution of this man who has already been the victim of police bungling to the extent of having a perjured witness put on the stand to testify against him.

"Second, I'll pull the covers off old Judge Tevis, no matter what time of night it is, and I'll explain what has happened. Judging from his mood today, I think I'll have no trouble getting him to sign a writ."

"You do what you want to do, counselor," said Romano in that flat, toneless voice, the voice of a man with a fixation, which Bart had heard earlier in the evening. "I'm taking this man down—in handcuffs."

Romano waved the young policeman away. The young man walked toward the glass door. Merusi, wearing handcuffs, was at his side. Marty drew Bart aside.

"Listen," he said, "I feel sure Romano will come to his senses. This shouldn't take more than an hour. This has been a busy day for Marty. I feel like going out on the town when it's finally over. Why don't you meet me later?"

Bart shook his head. He realized more than the others what Romano was doing. Romano was making the biggest mistake that any cop could make. He was getting tough at the wrong time. And he was already in serious trouble. Bart could not blame Land, but he wanted no more of Marty or Joe the Whistler. Not this evening, anyway.

"You play the upholstered gin mills, Marty," Bart said. "I like the ones with sawdust on the floor. I think I'll do my drinking at the Sligo Slasher's."

Marty said, "Suit yourself. Try to talk to Romano if you can. Maybe he'll listen to you. This can mean curtains for him, Hardin, coming right on top of what happened this morning. With any other cop in town I'd already be dropping dimes into the telephone and calling the District Attorney and if I couldn't get the District Attorney I'd call old Judge Tevis and if I couldn't get Tevis I'd damn well call the Police Commissioner or the Mayor. But I want to give Romano a chance to think, to reconsider. An hour or so in a back room won't hurt Joe the Whistler any. Romano's just a good man who's flipped his wig."

Marty hurried off after the policeman and his client. Men in white suits were putting the body of Benny Merusi on a stretcher. Their bustling movements had a gnome-like quality in this place of light and sprawling shadows and towering statuary. Romano stood apart, alone. His brooding eyes were on the sagging stretcher. His stocky figure seemed as grimly unyielding as the figure of Balzac on his pedestal.

Bart walked up to Romano. "Why do you think that Joe the Whistler killed his brother, Romano?" he asked.

Romano kept staring at the stretcher and its burden. Without looking at Bart, he said, "I know. I know he did, the same way that I know he killed Jason Breck."

Bart said, "If I hadn't testified in court this morning, Benny would be alive. Is that what you mean?"

Romano finally turned his head toward Bart. "Don't blame yourself," he said. "You had to testify. People always do what they've got to do. That's why I'm taking Joe the Whistler in. I've got to do it."

"It can mean trouble, Romano. Big trouble. You can be wrong. Marty's pulling his punches now, but he won't pull 'em long."

Romano said, "I know. I know what Marty is going to do. He's going to wait about an hour. He's going to give me Joe the Whistler for an hour. Maybe it'll be enough. Maybe I can make him talk. If I can't . . ."

He left it there.

Then suddenly Romano shook his head, as if he were coming out of a daze. "Butterfly," he said. "What the hell was it you were telling me about a butterfly?"

"Benny gave me a fingerpainting of a butterfly tonight," Bart answered.

"There's something I ought to remember about a butterfly," Romano declared. "But I don't. It's something to do with Joe the Whistler, too, I think. But I can't remember. Maybe I'm getting old. Maybe the Commissioner was right this afternoon when he kind of hinted I should retire and take my pension. You take a good look at this butterfly painting?"

Bart said, "I barely glanced at it. I didn't want to lug it around, so I left it up at Marty's house."

"Maybe I better take a look at it some time," Romano said. "Maybe it would jog my memory. There's something about a butterfly I ought to remember. It's just a kind of tickling inside my head."

"Marty's man is off today and Marty says he's going out on the town tonight when he finishes up with his client," Bart replied. "I couldn't get it for you before tomorrow."

"That's time enough," Romano answered. "It probably doesn't mean a thing. Marty won't destroy it. Marty's got lots of tricks, but he don't destroy evidence. He might push it behind a sofa pillow if he gets a chance, but he won't destroy it."

Bart suddenly remembered Benny's concern over the painting. He started to tell Romano, then he thought better of it. If the lieutenant knew that Joe the Whistler had wanted to destroy the butterfly, it might encourage him in his persecution of the man he had just sent away in handcuffs. He did not think the revelation could help Romano and he was afraid it might result in encouraging him to further folly.

As the men bearing the stretcher went by, Romano turned and followed them. His mind was obviously no longer occupied with the butterfly. Bart left the Sculpture Garden, walked through the museum and out into the street. He walked rapidly across town, turned down Eighth Avenue. On Forty-ninth Street, just west of Eighth, he turned into the Sligo Slasher's bar.

Tony Maclaren, the Sligo Slasher, claimed he had been the lightweight champion of Ireland in his youth and his place was filled with yellowing photographs and rusting trophies which he described fondly as "mementoes of the noble sport of Fistiana." The little bantam behind the bar and most of his customers were absorbed in watching the performance of an unusually tall, hawk-beaked man in a wide-brimmed Stetson who was manufacturing something he called a "depth bomb." A depth bomb apparently was made by dropping a shot of whisky, glass and all, into a glass of beer.

The hawk-beaked man dropped the small glass, bottom first, into the beer glass very carefully. "The principles of surface tension and osmosis are involved," he was explaining to the others. He consulted his watch. "You allow these chemical reactions to take place for exactly sixty seconds. During that time the spiritous liquor permeates the malt beverage slowly, drop by drop, and you finally have the most potent drink known to man."

After a minute had elapsed, he drank the mixture straight down as his audience applauded.

When Bart could finally attract Maclaren's attention away from the scientific experiment, he ordered a double Irish.

He suddenly felt the need of getting drunk as quickly as possible.

five

It is a bad thing to drink when you are bitter and Bart Hardin was the bitterest man in New York City on that raw November night.

Drinking did not improve his disposition. As he poured the Irish whisky down his throat his mood grew blacker and blacker. He assessed the results of his action that morning in testifying for a man called Joe the Whistler and he did not find them good.

He remembered an oft-repeated phrase from the years when he had served two hitches in the Marines: "Never volunteer." It was sound advice, he decided. He had made the great mistake of volunteering what he considered vital information to Marty Land, a lawyer who was defending a man on trial for his life. He hadn't liked the man on trial. From the first he had felt that Joe the Whistler was probably guilty of the murder of a good man and a respectable citizen named Jason Breck. Certainly Joe lived outside the law and profited enormously from doing so. He was importantly connected with a federation of wolves that exacted illegal tribute from the decent citizens of New York and did not stop at murder when murder was necessary to its purposes, even though the Syndicate was now organized along the lines of big business and did not engage in the blood baths that had marked the mobs of twenty years before.

Maybe it would have been better if he had let the perjured testimony of Busy Izzy stand. That, at least, would have resulted in the removal of one of the mob's sinister figures from society. The whole issue had been entirely dependent upon Bart Hardin. The other witnesses, Sleeth and Krenech and Merritt, had seemed to remember nothing of the incident at the card game until they were reminded. They would not have come forward voluntarily. That had been apparent.

But in America you simply didn't condemn a man to death or imprisonment on the testimony of a false witness, even though the man was guilty of a dozen other crimes. In a parallel case many years before, Vincent Coll, the "Mad Dog," had been set free by a judge when a perjured witness testified against him, even though every cop in town was convinced that he was guilty of the despicable Harlem baby-killings. Hardin had known for certain that the witness called Busy Izzy was lying and he had sworn to the truth as any man with decent instincts would do. Now he brooded bitterly on the results.

A man who had probably committed murder had been set free.

An older man for whom Hardin had felt a peculiarly warm friendship, a good cop and a fine human being, was in trouble, bad trouble. To make thinks worse, Romano was following the same pattern that many other outraged policemen had followed when they had been thwarted by obviously guilty hoodlums. He was going berserk. He was trying to wage a one-man war on crime, "fighting dirty," as he himself had called it. The whole department had sometimes successfully adopted a policy of reprisal and harassment against the mob's many enterprises, under such circumstances. But no cop could do it alone. The cops who had tried had almost always been dismissed from the force. That was very likely to happen to Romano.

Hardin himself had lost face on Broadway and it is as serious to lose face on Broadway as it is to lose face in the Orient. People were laughing behind his back. They believed he had sold out to the Syndicate or that the Syndicate had made him its unwitting stooge.

Finally, a harmless, dull-witted youth who had a quality of warmth and goodness in him had been brutally killed.

And all because I sat in a witness stand and told the truth, the whole truth and nothing but the truth, Hardin thought darkly.

Tony Maclaren, the little man who called himself the Sligo Slasher, sensed Hardin's black temper and did his best to dispel it. He told his most extravagant lies about his alleged career as the lightweight champion of the Emerald Isle. Hardin didn't laugh. He didn't even smile. He just drank double shots of whisky.

Eddie O'Grady, the Old Top Sarge, who served as lookout at Selig's book, came in and had a sarsaparilla. The Sarge

never drank hard liquor or even beer. The old man with the
mastiff face, who wore the Medal of Honor around his neck
in place of a tie, worshipped Hardin and he seemed to sense
that what he had said in the smoke shop that morning had
somehow offended his friend.

"Are you mad at me, Captain?" O'Grady asked like a perplexed child. "I don't know what it was I done, but I apologize."

Hardin tried to smile at the Sarge, but it didn't quite come
off. "You didn't do a thing, Sarge," he said. "You just reflected an attitude a little bit too accurately, and since I'm
sure you've got no idea at all what I'm talking about, you
may as well forget it."

The Old Sarge said, "I had a real good betting day on the
horses. I almost split even." He put change on the bar and
timidly asked Hardin to have a drink on him.

Bart shook his head curtly. He didn't want old Eddie to
spend his money buying him drinks. The Sarge needed it to
bet on longshots. When Bart refused the offer of the drink,
the Old Sarge left, crestfallen. Hardin realized he had made
another mistake. He should have accepted the drink. He had
hurt the old man by refusing.

It was a little after midnight and Hardin was · feeling
his liquor when Joe the Whistler walked into the bar. The
Whistler walked straight up to Bart. A silence fell over the
bar. Then a few of the more sycophantic Jacobs Beach characters greeted the Whistler and murmured congratulations
over his release from durance vile. They had not yet heard
of Benny's death. It had come too late for the bulldog editions of the tabs and Maclaren never tuned in anything but
sports events on his radio.

The Whistler acknowledged the greetings with curt nods.
He turned to Hardin and said, "I'm glad I found you. Marty
Land said you might be here. But I had to go home first and
put on decent clothes. Those bastards that picked me up
didn't even give me time to find my hat."

Hardin said, "I see you beat the rap again. I see Romano
didn't hold you."

The Whistler gave a short, unpleasant laugh that was more
like a phlegmy cough. "That clown Romano," he said. "He
thinks he's a character in *Dragnet* or something. It took about
half an hour altogether, maybe. Marty didn't even have to
call the D.A. or a judge. Romano didn't have a leg to stand

on and the big clown knew it. He played it real bad this time.

"When a murder squeal comes in he's supposed to notify the D.A. to send a man. Romano didn't. But the D.A. got wind of it somehow and he sent a man. He was there waiting for us. And you know who he was? That redhead Saltus, who prosecuted me in the Breck rap. Saltus was so upset when he saw me his freckles turned green. I guess he had his orders. I guess the D.A. was afraid Romano was going to screw things up worse than they were already. That Saltus was practically my mouthpiece. He had me out of there in nothing flat."

The Whistler signaled to Maclaren for a drink. He said, "What Romano had was absolutely nothing. A great big zero. Stephanie, Mrs. Breck, told 'em flat she'd been with me at the time poor Benny got chilled. One of the watchmen at the museum said Benny went out around eight-thirty for half an hour or so. He said he knocked at the service entrance to get in again. The watchman opened the door. There was somebody with Benny, but he was back in the shadows and the guard didn't see him good. He said Benny wanted to bring someone inside a minute and he told him it was all right and to lock the door as he was busy doing something else, so he went off and finished doing it."

Joe Merusi sipped his drink. "Nobody saw the guy who went in with Benny," he continued. "They must have walked right out to this kind of garden where Benny got killed. I guess the guy just walked right out again. I guess it was that simple. Nobody could describe the guy. I wish they could. I'd like to get my hands on the guy that killed Benny."

The Whistler gave Hardin a searching look. "Maybe you won't believe me," he said. "Maybe you think I'm too tough. But I loved my brother. We come up in the slums together. I always took care of him after he had the accident and hurt his head. I wanted to give him everything he needed after I got going good, but Marty Land said this job at the museum would make him feel important and make him happy, and he was right. Nobody should have killed poor Benny. There wasn't anything mean in him. He never hurt even a cockroach in his life. The only thing he ever did wrong was steal stuff for me or somebody he liked when he was a kid. Maybe it was wrong, but Benny never could figure it that way."

The funny part was that Bart believed Joe the Whistler had loved his brother, with the fierce, possessive, egotistic sort of love that mobsters often displayed toward their families. Hardin had never known a top hood who hadn't bought his old mother a big house and a Cadillac as soon as he hit the jackpot.

Hardin also was convinced that Joe the Whistler had killed his brother Benny.

Maclaren was standing in front of them, waiting for the Whistler's order. Joe said, "I'll take Scotch. Give my friend Mr. Hardin whatever he wants."

Hardin shook his head. "I don't want a drink," he said. "I like to drink alone."

The Whistler turned toward him, surprise and then anger on his dark face.

Maclaren sensed a situation. "Nobody's buying," he declared. "This one's on the house."

When the drinks were in front of them, Joe the Whistler said, "I guess you don't like me much, Hardin, since you don't want to drink with me. But the thing I come here for was to thank you for what you did this morning. You got out of court before I could see you and with that Romano leaning on me and my brother dead I couldn't say anything when I saw you at the museum. Thanks, Hardin. I mean that. Joe the Whistler don't forget a debt."

Hardin drank his whisky. He did not even look at his companion. "You haven't got a debt to remember. Not with me," he said.

Joe the Whistler was searching the dim barroom with his eyes. He said, "Listen, Hardin, there's something I've got to talk to you about. Something important. Is there a spot around here where we can be private?"

Maclaren had been hovering near by, ready to pour oil, Scotch or Irish on what was obviously troubled water. He said, "There's a back room with tables that nobody ever uses. The Slasher's customers like standing on their own two feet."

Bart said, "I've got nothing to talk to you about, Whistler. You're right. I don't like you very much. I just want to drink alone."

The Whistler was persistent. "Please, Hardin," he said. "This is important. Important to me and important as hell to you, too. Step back just a minute with me. You don't have to like me. Just listen to me, that's all."

Hardin could almost feel the eyes of the others at the bar regarding them covertly. He was half-drunk and he was suddenly enraged. Okay, he thought, let's give them something to talk about. It can't be worse than it is already.

He nodded, said to the Whistler, "Come on." He strode rapidly across the bar and pushed aside a curtain of the back room. There'll be new rumbles on Broadway tomorrow, he thought. Rumbles about Hardin's Syndicate connections.

The back room was dimly lighted. It had tables with checkered cloths. Hardin sat down at one of the tables. The Whistler sat across from him.

The Whistler's hard eyes scrutinized Hardin for a moment. There was no expression in them. Finally he said, "I've got something for you, Hardin. Don't look at it. Just stick it in your pocket and take it home."

He shoved a fat envelope across the table.

Hardin picked up the envelope and looked inside. It was fat with currency in high denominations.

Joe the Whistler said, "To save you counting, there's ten grand, Hardin. All in hundreds. There's more when you need it."

Hardin left the envelope lying on the table. He stood up and pushed his chair back. He said, "Stand up, Whistler."

Joe the Whistler shook his head. "No," he said. "I won't stand up."

Hardin walked around the table. "If you don't, you'll get it sitting down," he said.

The Whistler didn't move. He said, "Listen, Hardin, I won't stand up. You don't understand . . ."

Hardin's fist smashed hard into the Whistler's face.

The Whistler's chair overturned and he crashed heavily to the floor.

He lay on the floor, shaking his head and staring up at Hardin, the wreckage of the chair beneath him. Presently two crimson bubbles oozed slowly from the corner of his mouth.

The curtains parted and the Sligo Slasher came in, alarm written on his wizened face. "What's happening?" he asked. "What's happening in here?"

The Whistler said, "Nothing's happening. I just can't hold my booze. I fell out of the chair. Get out of here."

Maclaren looked questioningly at Hardin. Hardin inclined his head, dismissing him. The Slasher stood doubtfully for a moment, then he left and dropped the curtain.

The Whistler dabbed at his mouth with a handkerchief. "I won't get up, Hardin," he said. "Give me the boot if you want to, but I won't fight you. You saved my life and I won't fight you."

He looked at the blood on his fine linen handkerchief.
He said, "You don't understand. It wasn't a payoff for what
you did for me. I know you aren't for sale. Selig told me that.
I want to buy something from you, Hardin. That's what the
ten grand was for. If you want more, I'll pay it. I want to
make a buy, Hardin."

Hardin said, "Get up off the floor. I won't try to make
you fight."

The Whistler got to his feet. He kicked the splintered
chair into a corner, drew up another one, sat down. He held
the handkerchief to his broken mouth to stanch the blood.
He said, "I wish you hadn't hit me in the mouth. It makes
it hurt to talk."

"What do you want to buy, Whistler?" Bart asked. "I
haven't got anything worth ten grand."

The Whistler said, "The picture. I want to buy the picture
that my brother Benny gave you."

Hardin shook his head. "You've got it wrong, Whistler,"
he replied. "Benny didn't give me the picture he stole from
the museum, the one that is supposed to be so valuable.
He gave that to Marty Land and Marty returned it to a man
named Wainwright at the museum tonight. The picture
Benny gave me was one of his own fingerpaintings. It was a
picture of a butterfly."

There was a flicker of concern on the Whistler's face.
He said, "You looked at it?"

"I glanced at it, yes."

"It's all right. There's no harm done. I want to buy the
butterfly, Hardin. I'll pay ten grand or more if you want it."

"Why?" asked Bart.

"Benny was my brother. Maybe I'm sentimental."

"The butterfly has ten grand worth of sentimental value to
you?"

The Whistler nodded. "The money's on the table. If you
want more, name it."

Hardin's eyes narrowed. Perhaps Marty had told the Whistler about the butterfly, but that wasn't like Marty. When
Marty had a hood for a client he never told him any more
than he had to know. Mostly Marty's conversation with hoods
concerned the ways and means of collecting the large retainers
he demanded. And if Marty had been the source of the
Whistler's information, Joe must know the painting was at
Marty's house.

Hardin said, "How did you know Benny gave the picture to me?"

The Whistler's dead eyes were staring hard at Bart. "That chump Romano. He let it slip."

That added. "There's something about a butterfly," Romano had said. Maybe Romano had remembered what it was about a butterfly and had questioned the Whistler concerning the fingerpainting.

Bart said, "I don't have the painting. I left it up at Marty's house. There's no way of getting it. Marty's out on the town and won't be home before sunup."

"We'll find Marty," the Whistler declared. "I know the joints he plays. I even own a piece of some of them. You and me will go out on the town, too. We'll stay on the town till we find Marty and get the butterfly."

Bart shook his head. "There's something you haven't thought of, Whistler," he said.

"What?"

"I don't want to sell the butterfly."

There was real distress on Joe the Whistler's face now and he made no attempt to mask it.

He said, "Listen, Hardin, I'll level with you. I've got to have the butterfly. I've got to have it tonight. If ten grand's not enough, I've got a couple of more on me loose and I can get anything you want tomorrow when the bankroll for the book comes in. Just name it, Hardin, but let's get under way."

Hardin grinned and shook his head, "No, Whistler," he said. "The butterfly's not for sale. I told Marty to take good care of it for me. You couldn't get it from him, even if you are his client."

The Whistler sat very still for a moment. Despite his smashed mouth he was whistling tunelessly through his teeth. He always did that when he was under stress.

Finally he said, "I'm going to lay it on the table to you, Hardin. That butterfly's the hottest thing in town. You keep the butterfly, you don't stay healthy. Something real bad can happen to a man who's got the butterfly. I wouldn't want that you should be the man it happens to. You saved my life today."

Hardin thought for a minute, then he said, "Tell me why the butterfly is hot, Whistler. Tell me why you want it ten grand's worth. Maybe I'll consider if I know. Maybe I might sell."

A look of alacrity came into Joe the Whistler's face. He said, "So you don't know, then. That's just fine. That makes it perfect, Hardin. Perfect for you and me, too. Just pick up that envelope and we'll go out and find Marty and get the butterfly. And I tell you what. I just decided the price has doubled. Ten grand now and tomorrow at noon you drop by my place and pick up another envelope. There'll be ten gees in coarse notes inside. Okay?"

Bart smiled amiably at Joe the Whistler. "No," he said. "I've just decided I like the butterfly too well to sell. I may even get a frame for it sometime."

The Whistler's mouth was still bleeding slightly. He had dropped the bloodstained handkerchief on the table and he paid no attention to the crimson trickle that ran down his chin. There was fury and frustration on his face. "Listen, chum, you're talking real crazy," he said. "You're not in any penny-ante game. These boys play for yellow chips. There are certain people who want this butterfly and they'll do what they've got to do to get it. They'll do it to you or me or anybody, Hardin. This jackpot's too big for you. Throw in your cards while you're twenty grand ahead. Twenty grand can cover a lot of losing parlays, Hardin. And you buy yourself a flock of health insurance when you hand the butterfly to me."

Hardin shook his head and smiled. "No, Whistler, I'm very fond of butterflies. It's not for sale."

Joe the Whistler was a gambler. He knew better than to argue about a losing bet. He picked up the envelope stuffed with money.

He rose and shook his head at Hardin. He wiped the blood from his chin with the back of his hand. He hadn't bothered to pick up the stained handkerchief from the table.

The Whistler said, "I'm sorry, Hardin. Maybe you don't believe it, but I tried hard to stop what's going to happen. I owe you something for what you did down in the courthouse and I like to pay my debts." He fished in his pocket, brought out a small card, pushed it in Hardin's direction. "There's my private phone number," he said. "If you change your mind, call me up, no matter what time it is."

He started toward the door, then he turned toward Hardin again. "Maybe it's too bad I wouldn't fight you," he said. "I could clobber you any time. Maybe I could have beat some sense into your head."

"With your blackjack?" Hardin asked.

The Whistler said, "So long, Hardin. Nice seeing you."

As he pushed aside the curtain he was whistling through his teeth.

For once, Hardin could recognize the tune.

Joe was whistling the famous aria "One Fine Day," from Puccini's opera, *Madame Butterfly*.

six

Joe the Whistler walked hurriedly through the bar and out into the street, still whistling through his teeth.

He stood outside the Sligo Slasher's for a moment, looking at the door. When Hardin did not emerge, the Whistler walked a few yards down the dark street and joined two men who were standing in front of a second-hand electrical-appliance store pretending to examine small-screen television sets that had become antiques in a single decade of electronic progress.

The Whistler said to one of the men, "You think this Hardin would make you, Charley?"

The man shook his head. "He's seen me around on the Beach, maybe, a time or two, but he don't know me."

"Watch the bar, then," the Whistler said. "When he comes out, tail him. When he goes into that flat of his on Forty-second above the flea circus, call in. You've got the number."

Charley nodded. "I know," he said. "I just call, that's all?"

The Whistler nodded and turned to the other man. "You know that house that Marty Land, the Mouth, owns up on Sixtieth?"

The second man said he knew.

"Get up there. Hang around until Marty Land shows up. He's out somewhere now getting stinko and it may be a long time. But call in the minute he goes in his house, no matter what time it is. You understand?"

The second man nodded.

A passing car threw light on Joe the Whistler's face.

Charley said, "Hey, boss! You got a fat lip. This Hardin give you that? Is this going to be a muscle job before it's finished?"

Joe the Whistler shook his head. "No muscle," he answered. "Tonight we're chasing butterflies, that's all."

The Whistler walked away. The man named Charley took a post where he could see the door of Maclaren's bar without being seen himself. The other man hesitated a moment, then shrugged and began to walk east.

Hardin remained at the table in the back room of the Sligo Slasher's for several minutes after Joe the Whistler left. He caressed the knuckles of his left hand, which had been slightly bruised by the blow to Joe the Whistler's mouth. The punch hadn't hurt the Whistler too much, he thought. The Whistler still could whistle. Presently Hardin rose, pushed aside the curtains and went into the bar.

Maclaren came around the bar and hurried up to him. "I see you hung one on his kisser," he said in a husky whisper. "Was it the old left hook? Did you remember what I told you, to give that little twist to the elbow and the wrist? That's what does it. The old Maclaren corkscrew. It sent Slamming Sammy Silks into the laps of the ringside customers on St. Patrick's Day of 1918."

Hardin grinned, said, "The Whistler can't hold his liquor. He fell right out of his chair."

He went into a phone booth. On an off chance he dialed the number of Marty Land's home. The phone rang a long time. There was no answer.

Hardin thought a minute. He'd get claustrophobia if he stood in the phone long enough to call all the spots where Marty might be tonight. He left the booth, had another Irish at the bar. Then he nodded good night to Maclaren and walked out to the street. As he turned uptown to Eighth Avenue he did not notice the man who had moved out of the shadows to follow him.

Hardin walked two blocks to the old firehouse where the *Broadway Times* was published. The doors of the newspaper office were never locked. There wasn't much to steal except the typewriters and they were valuable mainly as vintage specimens. Maddox Slade, the socially pretentious owner of the sports and theatrical paper, believed fondly that the office was used as a kind of informal club by Broadway night owls, the interesting people who made theatre news. It had been once, many years before, but it wasn't now, not on this racket-ridden Big Street of the 1950's with its deadfalls and sucker traps and boardwalk concessionaires. Sometimes a drunk came in to sleep it off and occasionally one of the younger Broadway reporters brought a girl there for a necking party in the cavernous interior of the old building. Usually old Tim Dargan, the watchman, was the only occupant of the place after the last editions of the *Broadway Times* hit the street around eight o'clock. He was the only occupant of the building now.

Tim was sitting at the phone desk, eating sandwiches from a lunch box and drinking coffee from a thermos bottle when Hardin entered.

Hardin said, "Hello, Tim, how's your missus coming along?"

"Mr. Bart!" the old man exclaimed, rising to his feet and extending his hand. "I haven't seen you in a week. I wanted to tell you. The doctor says she's going to be all right. She's going to get well! It's all because of you, Mr. Bart. If you hadn't given me that five hundred for the operation last September I don't know what we would have done. . . ."

"Nuts," Bart interrupted him brusquely. "I told you I didn't give it to you. You and I just played a number together and it came up. Lady Luck and the numbers bank paid for the operation, Tim."

"But I didn't tell you to play the number for me, Mr. Bart. I didn't even give the dollar to you. I'm going to pay you back, a little at a time, just as soon as there aren't so many bills for medicine and doctor's calls and all. . . ."

"You'll pay me nothing," Bart said shortly. "You and I played 312 together in the numbers pool September eighth and it won and we split the winnings. Move over, Tim, I want to plug my phone in to an outside line."

Bart leaned across the phone desk and plugged in the line on the board. He patted old Tim's shoulder and walked toward the city room. The watchman's voice followed him. "God bless you, Mr. Bart. You saved her life."

If I did, Hardin thought as he walked toward his cubbyhole office, at least it was a life worth saving. I'm not so sure about the other life they claim I saved.

Hardin sat down at the rolltop desk, pulled the phone toward him. He consulted a directory of night clubs on the desk and began to dial numbers. During the next fifteen or twenty minutes he dialed the numbers of eleven night spots, most of them exclusive and expensive places on the east side of Manhattan. Marty Land was known in all of them, but he had been in none of them during the evening. Finally Bart dialed the number of Marty's house again. Once more the phone rang a long time and once more there was no answer.

When Bart finally hung up, he sat for a few minutes tapping his fingers on the desk and thinking. There wasn't much more he could do tonight unless he was able to get the butterfly from Marty and he didn't quite know what he would do if he got the butterfly. He didn't think he would be able to reach Marty before morning. Marty had evidently changed his mind about going out on the town and hitting the spots. If that had been his program he almost certainly would have been in one of the places Bart had called. Marty was a bachelor and he had the addresses of certain pretty ladies who lived in apartment houses where the staffs were discreet. It was highly probable that Marty wouldn't be home until morning. Rather late in the morning, in all likelihood.

Bart looked at his watch. It was nearly one-thirty now. He left the old building and walked down Eighth Avenue. At Forty-ninth he paused uncertainly, debating whether he would go back to the Sligo Slasher's and continue his conscientious effort to get drunk, which had been interrupted by Joe the Whistler. He never went to bed until the spots closed at four o'clock, anyway. But he decided that he might need a clear head for tomorrow, now that the blue-jowled muggs of Broadway were mysteriously and ludicrously engaged in a butterfly chase. He decided to go home and try to get some sleep. After all, he had risen before his usual hour that morning. He had been in court at ten o'clock. His duties on the *Broadway Times* did not begin until noon.

He walked on south toward Forty-second, past dance halls and gin mills and tawdry motion picture houses and buildings that advertised ROOMS in large electric lights. A group of beer-dazed sailors in front of a chop suey parlor debated whether they would go in and eat chicken chow mein or continue their search for girls. A woman with restless eyes looked as if she were about to accost him, then suddenly changed her mind. Doors swung open and spilled clamorous juke-box rock-'n'-roll into the street.

At Forty-second, Bart turned east.

The man named Charley, who had been following Hardin at a distance, turned east, too. Hardin went into a battered brick building on the south side of the street near Broadway. A large neon sign reading BROMBERG'S FLEA CIRCUS AND FUN ARCADE belted the building. Hardin's shadow remained on the north side of the street. Charley waited a few minutes after Hardin entered the place, then he went into a nearby bar, entered a phone booth and dialed the number he had been given.

When there was an answer, he said two words: "Hardin's home."

Hardin climbed two flights of stairs, past the shooting gallery and amusement parlor on the street floor and the flea circus on the second. He unlocked the door of his flat, switched on lights. The old-fashioned living room was shadowy and cavernous. As usual, two dead-white nude figures seemed to leap out of the gloom at him. They were marble figures of Atlas and they supported the mantel over his fireplace. Hardin had named them Klaw and Erlanger after the theatrical producers of another era. Now they reminded him of the statuary in the Sculpture Garden of the museum, of the figure of Balzac, standing haughtily in his furled cloak, with wide-eyed Benny Merusi staring up at him unbelievingly.

Without removing his coat or hat, Hardin sat down beside the telephone. He took a scribbled list of phone numbers he had copied at the office from his pocket. He began to call night clubs again and ask for Marty Land. Marty wasn't in the first three clubs he called. He had just begun to dial the fourth, when there was a knock on his door. Because the street door entered upon the fun arcade and flea circus as well as the flats above, it was never locked.

Hardin had left messages at the clubs to have Marty call him. Perhaps Marty had decided to appear in person instead. Hardin crossed to the door and opened it.

Outside the door were two men who had long been dead.

One of them was Adolf Hitler.

The other was Benito Mussolini.

Adolf Hitler had a gun in his hand and it was pointed straight at Bart's stomach. The gun nudged Hardin, forced him to step back inside the room.

Adolf Hitler and Benito Mussolini entered, closing the door behind them and locking it with the key Bart had inserted on the inside of the lock when he entered the room.

Hardin looked at the two men and realized it would be impossible to describe them to the police, if he lived to describe them. They not only wore rubber masks that covered their entire faces. Their hat brims were pulled down so far that he could not even tell if their hair was dark or light. It wasn't raining, but both men wore long, dark rubber coats that hung almost to their ankles. Even their hands were concealed by gloves.

Neither man spoke a word, but Bart noted with ironic amusement that they seemed to have some respect for historical accuracy. The rubber-faced Hitler was obviously the boss, the one who gave the orders. He forced Bart into the chair he had just vacated, indicated he should place his hands in full view on the table beside him. Hitler picked up the telephone and placed it out of reach on the floor. He nodded to Mussolini, who at once began an exhaustive search of the apartment. Hitler stood a few feet from Bart, the gun held loosely in his hand. The rubber caricature of Hitler's face, with its Charlie Chaplin mustache, smirked down at Hardin. Bart decided that neither man was tall enough nor heavy enough to be Joe the Whistler.

Bart recalled what the Whistler had told him:

"There are certain people who want this butterfly and they'll do what they've got to do to get it. . . . Something real bad can happen to the man who's got the butterfly."

The search went on systematically and silently. The rubber face of Hitler stared at Bart as impassively as the marble faces of Klaw and Erlanger.

Presently Mussolini emerged from the bedroom. He had found the fingerpaintings Benny had bestowed on Hardin beneath the stack of soiled clothing Bart had neglected to send to the laundry. Hitler handed the gun to Mussolini, who kept it pointed at Bart. Hitler examined the half-dozen brightly colored cardboards. He shook his head, shrugged.

For the first time, someone spoke.

"If you're looking for the butterfly it isn't here," Hardin said. "I told Joe the Whistler I didn't have it."

Neither Hitler nor Mussolini responded. They had evidently decided to take Benny's fingerpaintings anyway. Perhaps they thought one of Benny's abstract designs resembled a butterfly. Mussolini handed the gun back to Hitler and put the paintings under his arm. He searched his pocket, brought out some stout cord and turned toward Hitler.

Hitler went to the door. He tested the lock, saw it was the kind that had to be locked by turning the key on the outside. He shook his head and Mussolini put the cord back in his pocket.

Hitler and Mussolini walked toward the door.

The whole business had taken less than half an hour. The apartment was a shambles. Bart's possessions were strewn over the floor. Even the bed in the other room had been taken apart.

Hitler took the key from the lock. Mussolini walked out and Hitler followed. Hardin heard the key turn.

There was only one door that led to the hallway. Hardin crossed rapidly to the front window. The streaked panes glowed rosily from the neon sign of Bromberg's flea circus. There was a fire escape outside the window. Hardin raised the window and stepped out on the fire escape. By the time he reached the railing, the men in the long black raincoats were hurrying out of the building. He could only see their backs and could not tell if they were still wearing the rubber masks. A car was parked almost directly in front of the door. There was a driver in the car. The door was open and the motor running. Bart could see the driver only as a large bulk in the front seat. The two men got into the car, slammed the door. The car roared off. Bart could not see the license number. He suspected it was a stolen plate anyway. The car was a dark De Soto, not a new model. There were lots of cars like that.

Hardin saw no reason to make a spectacle of himself before the crowds that still thronged Times Square by climbing down the fire escape. He had known it was useless to try to shout above the noise of traffic on the street, to make anyone understand that he should try to stop the men in the instant before the car sped away. He went back into the room, picked up the telephone and called Bromberg, who was his landlord as well as proprietor of the flea circus. He had left a key to the apartment with Bromberg in case of emergency.

Bart told Bromberg some drunken friends had played a joke and locked him in the apartment. Bromberg, a small, expostulative, chubby man with a spit curl, appeared presently and unlocked the door. He told Bart that the jokers had taken the key with them.

"Fine friends you got," Bromberg declared. "Maybe I should leave you locked up tight. It would keep you from drinking Irishman's whisky and getting into trouble. Crazy pipple doing crazy things, that's all Bromberg ever gets in this house. What crazy pipple locked you up and took your key away?"

"Two guys named Hitler and Mussolini," Bart told him.

Bromberg nodded. "I believe you," he said. "In this house I would believe it if I saw the Statue of Liberty walking up the stairs in a Bikini bathing suit."

Bromberg left Bart the key to the apartment, and departed, muttering darkly over the vicissitudes of a Broadway landlord.

Hardin thought of calling the police and decided against it. He didn't think there was anything the police could do. A description of two men who looked like Hitler and Mussolini wearing dark raincoats was highly inadequate. He had debated earlier whether he should call Romano and tell him that Joe the Whistler wanted the fingerpainting so much that he would pay ten thousand, even twenty thousand, dollars for it. He had decided against that, too. It might serve to jog Romano's memory, to make him recall the thing he had forgotten about the butterfly. It was more likely to encourage the lieutenant to further foolish acts and it would be regrettable indeed if Romano had more foolish acts written on his record now.

The butterfly, he decided, was safe enough. Marty Land owned valuable paintings and other possessions and his house was well secured against burglary and was protected by the Holmes Agency. Bart knew for certain that Joe the Whistler could not talk Marty out of the butterfly. And he thought it most unlikely that Marty would make his unsteady way home before breakfast.

Hardin looked at his watch. It was nearly two-thirty in the morning. He decided to pick up the scattered bedclothes, make his bed and try to get some sleep. He had just completed a sketchy job of tucking in the sheets and blankets that his visitors had torn asunder when his phone rang.

There was an extension phone beside the bed and Bart picked it up. He said, "Hardin speaking."

The voice on the other end of the wire was feminine, husky and theatrical. It said, "This is Stephanie Breck, Mr. Hardin. I have to see you right away. I know it's very late, but believe me, it's urgent. Can you come up here to my house on Fifty-sixth Street?"

seven

If Eddie O'Grady, the Old Top Sarge, hadn't been a horse-player, he might have saved himself a split head.

As he walked east on Forty-ninth Street seeking a taxicab, he came within yards of Bart Hardin just as he neared Broadway, but he didn't see him. He didn't see him because he was playing the horseplayers' favorite game, the game of might-have-been, and he was virtually unconscious of the world around him. The Old Sarge was trying to add up in his head how much money he'd have had *if* all the horses he'd bet in if-reverse parlays the afternoon before had won instead of losing and *if* Moe Selig hadn't had a ceiling limit on parlay pay-offs, anyway. The if-reverse and such variants of it as the round-robin and the birdcage are involved betting systems in which money on possible winners is reinvested on horses that may already have lost hours before and only the surrealistic mathematics of horseplayers could ever possibly have conceived them to begin with. The Old Sarge had arrived at a satis-factorily astronomical sum about the time that Hardin passed within a few feet of him, walking fast and headed uptown. The Sarge had never got beyond the seventh grade in school and he had learned higher mathematics by figuring betting odds. This problem was too much for him, however, he decided. He doubted he could even do it with pencil and paper. He'd have to refer it to Figures Phil Klein, a mathematical wizard who served as a cashier for Selig's book. Figures Phil could multiply sixteen numbers by sixteen numbers in his head and give you the answer faster than Nashua could run a furlong.

If the Old Sarge had ever lucked into one of his impossible parlays, he would hardly have changed his way of life at all. He was a compulsive horseplayer, and like all compulsive horseplayers he thought of money as something that you re-

68

invest on the chances of another horse on another day. He
finally found a vacant cab on the east side of Broadway. By
that time, Hardin had reached Fiftieth Street and the Sarge's
mental mathematics had soared to the point where he was
betting $37,000 on a 17 to 1 shot.

Hardin had tried to stall Stephanie Breck on the phone, to
discover what she wanted with him at two-thirty o'clock in the
morning. Most men, he thought wryly, would not have inquired about her motives. They would have rushed to the
house on Fifty-sixth, piously hoping that her intentions were
strictly dishonorable. Stephanie was no longer a starlet who
served as Hollywood's greatest gift to pin-up calendar art.
During the half-dozen years she had been married to Jason
Breck her pictures had appeared more frequently in society
columns than they had on barbershop walls. She had been a
patroness for numerous benefit balls and dramatic performances for the Actors' Fund. Her name had also appeared in
Broadway columns from time to time coupled suggestively
with the names of Broadway playboys and, more recently, the
name of the Syndicate bookmaker, Joe the Whistler.

Stephanie had proved very good indeed at verbal fencing
and at intriguing Bart's interest. She had told him only that
she had to see him at the earliest possible moment, that the
matter was of the greatest urgency both to him and to herself, that she was in serious trouble and that he was the only
man in New York City who could help her.

Hardin had finally consented, but he had decided to walk
the fairly long distance to the Breck house instead of taking a
cab. He had wanted a little time to think. He had been so
preoccupied that he had not noticed the man named Charley
who was lingering across the street from the flea circus when
he left his house. Charley had gone immediately into a bar,
dialed a number and once again had said two words: "Hardin's
left."

Bart hadn't seen the Old Sarge approaching as he crossed
Forty-ninth, either. He would have been surprised to find the
Old Sarge abroad at this hour of the morning. Ordinarily,
Eddie O'Grady should have been cloistered in his furnished
room handicapping the past performances for the next day's
races.

Hardin couldn't figure out the move on Stephanie's part,
except that he felt sure Joe the Whistler was behind it. There
didn't seem to be much point in merely luring him from his
flat so they could search it again, even though they now had a

key. They must have satisfied themselves already that the
butterfly wasn't hidden in the apartment above the flea circus.
There was always that chance that he was walking into a trap,
of course. But that didn't seem to add, either. If Joe the Whistler was going to get violent, in all likelihood he would have
used Hitler and Mussolini for his purposes. It hardly seemed
likely he would choose his girl friend's house as a place where
he would have Hardin beaten or murdered. It didn't make
much sense—the perjured witness, Benny's death, especially
the grim determination of Broadway mobsters to procure a
picture of a butterfly that a mentally deficient youth had
daubed upon a piece of board with his fingers.

Nick Carter and the Great Butterfly Chase, he thought, as
he turned east on Fifty-sixth.

Near Fifth Avenue were two elegant graystone houses that
had once belonged to a famous New York family. One of
them was now Jason Breck's Flower Garden night club and
it was doing business as usual despite the murder of its owner.
The façade of the club had been renovated with a stark and
striking modern combination of glass and stone and chromium
and there was an awning and a uniformed doorman. The twin
house next door was the Breck residence. Its Regency front
had not been altered. Bart mounted steps and rang the bell.

Stephanie answered the bell.

Hardin had met her several times at opening nights and
theatrical gatherings, although he had never really known her.
The evening gowns she had worn on those occasions had been
far more revealing than the negligee she wore now. But the
negligee, Stephanie's attitude, her tone of voice, the words she
spoke in greeting, somehow managed to convey an air of intimacy hardly warranted by her casual acquaintance with
Hardin.

"Please come in," she said. "We're quite alone. No one will
disturb us, Mr. Hardin."

The hallway was dimly lighted. She led Bart through it into
a large living room furnished with handsome traditional pieces
and sheltered from the world by rich and heavy draperies. Bart
was noticing the woman more than her surroundings. She
must be around thirty now, he thought, remembering that she
had been a young kid some talent scout had picked up from
behind a perfume counter when she first went to Hollywood
ten years before. Maturity became her. It had rounded out a
figure that had been lush enough to begin with. Her dark hair
was cut in Italian gamin style, very short, and it emphasized

the fine shape of her small head, the face that still seemed beguilingly immature despite the hard look in the very deep blue eyes under the contrived arches of the brows. The mouth was full and appealingly petulant.

Stephanie Breck said, "Sit down, Mr. Hardin. It's good to have you here. Frankly, I'm afraid. I'm in a mess. There's no use in being coy with you. I suppose you know that I'm the kind of woman who's always in some kind of a mess. But this one is particularly bad and oddly enough, you're the only person on earth who can help me out of it. Wait. I'll get us drinks first. Is Scotch all right?"

Hardin nodded. The trouble with drinking Irish was that not many people kept it in their homes.

Stephanie left the room. Bart arose and looked at a collection of miniatures painted on porcelain that were on the mantelpiece. He thought he recognized one of the ladies as Madame Pompadour and another as Napoleon's empress, Josephine. He was examining one of the miniatures when Stephanie returned with the drinks. It was a painting of a very lovely woman with long curls and violet eyes. She wore a tiara and, strangely, there was also a wispy scarf wrapped over her head and around her neck. The scarf flew out to her left as if wind were blowing it.

Stephanie drew close to him. He could smell her perfume. She was staring at the miniature and when she spoke Bart thought that there was something closely akin to fright in her voice.

"Why are you looking at that?" she demanded.

Bart put the miniature back on the mantelpiece. "No reason," he said. "She's a pretty lady, that's all."

"It's Louise of Austria," Stephanie said, and there was an odd note of challenge in her voice.

Bart said, "Austrian women have the reputation of being beautiful. You're Hungarian yourself, aren't you?"

Stephanie said, "There's some truth in that. My mother was Hungarian. My father wasn't. I was born in Brooklyn. The Stephanie story is largely a Hollywood press agent's myth, of course."

Bart sat down and accepted a drink.

"You know about Louise of Austria, Mr. Hardin?" Stephanie asked.

Bart shook his head.

"I thought you might, because of your interest in the miniature. She was a great beauty but her neck was horribly swollen by a goiter. She always wore something to cover her neck when she had her picture painted and most of the great artists of her time painted her. In this one she is wearing a scarf."

Bart sipped his drink, said, "I see."

"I collect historic jewelry, you know," Stephanie continued, sitting down near Bart. "A few of the ladies who once owned the jewelry are on the mantelpiece. That's why I collected the miniatures. Nearly all those women influenced history because they were beautiful. I get a kind of kick I can't explain out of wearing the bracelets and ear-drops and necklaces that touched their flesh centuries ago. Does that make me seem kind of queer to you, Mr. Hardin?"

Bart said, "No. Most beautiful women like jewelry. Also they like power, I suppose."

Stephanie set her drink down, rose, stood in front of the mantel, looking silently at Hardin. Finally she said, "Do you think I'm beautiful, Hardin? Most men do."

"Yes," said Bart. "I think you're beautiful."

Stephanie bit her full, bright mouth, stared at Hardin a long while. Then she said, "What do you want, Hardin? Joe says you don't want money."

"I like money," Hardin replied. "Only I'd rather earn it honestly, like betting on a winner or making Little Joe the hard way."

"Why do you want that damned butterfly? It can't possibly mean anything to you."

Hardin finished his drink before he answered.

"A friend of mine painted the butterfly," he answered. "He died a rather nasty death a few hours ago."

"Oh, come, now, Hardin! Don't tell me you're soft and sweet and sentimental. Don't tell me you're turning down thousands of dollars for a perfectly worthless object just because you treasure a dead boy's memory. You've got the reputation around the Street of being a pretty hard-boiled guy."

Hardin said, "If I knew why you and the Whistler want the butterfly I might be tempted to sell."

"Why do you have to know?" Stephanie asked. "What possible difference can it make? It's worthless to you and it's worth a lot to somebody else. That's all you've got to know. Just name your price and sell it."

Hardin thought for a moment and when he spoke, his words came slowly. "Maybe I could understand the Whistler wanting the butterfly," he said. "Maybe it's tied up in some way I don't understand with the murder of Benny or even with the murder

of your husband. But why should you call me up in the middle
of the night? Why should you want it, Stephanie? Is it just
because Joe told you to get it from me?"

Stephanie clutched the arms of her chair. Her body was
thrust forward, tense and trembling. "I've got to have it, Hardin," she said. "I've got to have it tonight. That damn-fool
thing can ruin me."

She sat leaning toward Hardin for a moment, her hard blue
eyes holding his. The negligee slipped away from one of the
bare legs that had helped to make her Hollywood's favorite
model for calendar art. She said, "I'll pay anything I have to
pay, Hardin. Anything."

Hardin spoke quite casually. He said, "Did you kill your
husband, Stephanie? Is that why you have to have the butterfly?"

Stephanie sprang from the chair. She stood over Hardin,
the fingers of her right hand curled as if she were about to
rake his face with the sharp red nails. "You louse!" she said.
"You filthy, rotten louse!"

"*Did* you kill him, Stephanie?" Hardin asked calmly.

Stephanie Breck collapsed into the chair again. She threw
back her head and closed her eyes. She said, "No. I didn't kill
him. I didn't love him. I'm something of a tramp and I
cheated on him, but I didn't kill him. I married him for his
money. I wanted the position, the security he could give me.
I was slipping in Hollywood. I was the best cheesecake the
studio had, but something funny is happening in Hollywood.
Today actresses who make it have to know how to act. They
can't go on forever posing for publicity stills. I can't act and I
always knew it. Breck came along and wanted me and it was
the way out. Sometimes I hated him. He was a man who
bought beautiful girls for his night club and his bed the same
way other rich men buy foreign sports cars or old masters. I
was his fourth wife, you know."

Hardin didn't answer her. She sat limply, leaning her head
back against the chair, her eyes still closed. She said, "Sometimes I thought I would divorce him and get alimony like the
others did, but he wasn't tired of me yet. He let the others
divorce him because he was tired of them. He wanted to keep
me. He knew about the other men, about Joe in particular,
but he wanted to keep me just the same. And he had enough
power to keep me. I could never have got a divorce if he
hadn't wanted it."

"How did you get mixed up with a cheap bookmaker, a

mobster like the Whistler, Stephanie?" Hardin asked. "You're still considered a very glamorous lady. Your marriage gave you wealth and social position. You must have had your choice of many men. Why Joe?"

"He was exciting," Stephanie said. "He took what he wanted no matter what he had to do to get it. I liked that. Jason was ruthless, too, in a different way. He was secure. He always played it according to the book. But Joe didn't. Joe lived dangerously. He took chances. And he was violent. I like violent men. They fascinate me."

The blue eyes opened and scrutinized Hardin provocatively. "I think you're a violent man, Hardin," Stephanie said. "That was quite a lump you put on poor Joe's lip tonight."

Hardin said, "What happened here the night your husband was murdered, Stephanie?"

"I told the truth to the District Attorney," she replied. "Joe didn't murder Jason, at least I don't think he did. You must believe that he is innocent. You testified for him. I had been feeling rather ill. I went to bed much earlier than usual. It must have been between two-thirty and three o'clock that I was awakened by a noise. At first I thought it was Jason coming in from the Flower Garden next door. Then I realized the noise came from my dressing room. The only servant who sleeps in was in bed in the back of the house. I went to the dressing room. I saw a man's back going out the door. It was dark and I couldn't describe him. I barely saw his back. I heard him running down the stairs and I started screaming. Then I heard a shot. When I got downstairs the man had gone and Jason was lying there on the floor dead, with a bullet in him. The man had taken a jewel box from my dressing room, a very large jewel box. It contained a few fairly valuable modern pieces, but mostly it was filled with replicas of the antique jewelry I collect. The real jewelry was in a bank vault, of course. I wore the real jewels on important occasions but I kept the paste replicas for more casual affairs. Most women who own valuable jewels do that, of course. It was just a common burglary. The thief thought he had the real jewels. The paste replicas never have shown up. But the police arrested Joe and tried to frame him with this witness they'd hired. They might have got away with it if it hadn't been for you."

"And now you want the butterfly," Hardin said.

"Yes," said Stephanie, "I've got to have the butterfly. Just as quickly as I can get it. It's got nothing to do with Jason's murder, Hardin. Believe me, the less you know about it, the better off you are. I can't explain it. It would involve you in something that doesn't concern you. Will you get the butterfly for me, Hardin?"

Bart said, "Do you want the butterfly for Joe the Whistler, Stephanie?"

Stephanie shook her head. She rose from the chair, stood very close to Hardin. If he had moved only slightly his hand would have touched her. Stephanie said, "I want it for myself, Hardin. That's why I'm making you the offer."

"Just what is your offer?" Bart asked.

Stephanie's hand pressed his shoulder, turned him gently toward her. When he looked up into her face, she said, "Is that the way you get your kicks, Hardin, by humiliating people, by making them crawl? Are you going to make me spell it out for you? I told you you could name your price."

Bart shook his head at her. "Joe must be desperate," he said, "to make you do a thing like this."

"Damn you, Hardin!" she flared. "Can't you understand that it's for me? Joe tried to get it because of me. He couldn't buy it from you at any price. That's why I called you. That's why I'm doing this. Can't you understand?"

Hardin rose from the chair and walked away from her. He toyed with one of the porcelain miniatures on the mantelpiece.

"Were the men in rubber masks who pulled a gun on me tonight also acting in your behalf?" he asked.

"I don't know about that, Hardin. Believe me, I don't. But I know you're asking for trouble if you keep the thing. Until I get it and destroy it I'm in trouble, too. I don't scare easy, but I'm scared to death right now. That's why I'll do anything to get the butterfly."

Hardin turned and faced her. "Anything?" he asked.

Her eyes met his steadily. "Anything, Hardin. I told you that."

Hardin said, "Tell me why you want it. Tell me the truth and maybe I'll name my price."

"No, Hardin. That's the one thing I can't do."

Hardin shrugged. He stubbed out a cigarette in an ash tray. He picked up his glass and finished his drink. He said, "In that case, the butterfly is not for sale. Thanks for the Scotch." He started toward the hall.

Stephanie cried, "Wait, Hardin! For God's sake don't leave me alone here!"

There was a sudden, clamorous sound in the room. The telephone was ringing.

Stephanie said, "Wait. Please wait just a minute."

She picked up the telephone.

Hardin looked at his watch. It was twenty after three.

Stephanie said "Hello" into the phone. Then she listened for several moments. The expression on her face was completely inscrutable. Finally she said, "No. I'm afraid you have the wrong number."

She turned slowly toward Bart. There was a little smile on her lips now. She seemed entirely at ease in contrast to her emotional state of a moment before.

She said, "I'm sorry you have to leave, Hardin. It rather wounds my pride to have my offer spurned so rudely. I suppose all women who believe they're beautiful overrate their appeal to men. Thanks for coming, anyway. Good night, Hardin."

Hardin said, "That's all?"

There was open, contemptuous amusement on Stephanie's face. She smiled at Hardin. "What else?" she asked. "You're a noble character, Hardin. Completely incorruptible. My late husband would have admired you. He was like that, too."

"You're not afraid to be alone now?" Hardin asked. "Just a minute ago you said you were scared to death."

"There's a servant asleep upstairs," she answered, smiling with ironic sweetness. "It's good of you to be concerned, but I'll be quite all right. A woman scorned should at least be granted the privilege of licking her wounds in solitude."

Hardin didn't answer. He walked to the hall and got his coat and hat. As he was opening the street door he heard her soft laughter behind him. "Good night again, Hardin," said Stephanie Breck. "It might have been fun, you know."

Hardin walked out and shut the door behind him.

He had to walk four blocks before he could find a bar that was open. In this area many of the gin mills closed at midnight. When he found a bar on Sixth Avenue that was still lighted, he entered and went immediately to the phone booth. He dialed Marty Land's number. The phone rang and rang. There was still no answer.

Hardin found a vacant cab and directed the driver to the flea circus on Forty-second Street.

When he went into his flat the scene of air-raid chaos that the rubber-faced Hitler and Mussolini had left was depressing, but Hardin made no attempt to clean up the disarray.

He still hoped that Marty might get the message he had left at eleven clubs and call him.

He showered and went to bed, finally. He noted that he'd stayed up until the legal closing hour of the gin mills, anyway. It was after four o'clock.

He slept for only a little while. Shortly before six o'clock, when a dirty gray November dawn was thrusting into the canyon of Times Square, his phone rang.

A crisp voice told the sleepy Hardin that the emergency ward of City Hospital was calling.

"There's a man here suffering from concussion and possible fracture of the skull," the voice said. " His name is Eddie O'Grady. Do you know him, Mr. Hardin?"

Hardin told the caller that he knew the Old Sarge, asked what had happened.

"He was apparently the victim of assault," the voice replied. "He was picked up unconscious some hours ago. He has just regained consciousness and he refuses to remain here unless he sees you. He requires treatment and it is not wise to give him too much sedation. He is partly delirious, apparently. He keeps calling for you and muttering something about a butter-fly."

eight

The Old Sarge lay on a small cot in the overcrowded hospital ward. His head was swathed in a great white turban of bandages. As the Sarge looked up at Bart there was a stricken expression on his grizzled face and his mouth quivered as if he were about to burst into tears. In the next bed a huge Negro moaned in agony. He was encased in plaster like a mummy. Across the way a sleepless old man with dazed, staring eyes kept murmuring, "Martha? Martha? They took away my false teeth, Martha!"

The Old Sarge said, "I failed you, Captain. I didn't accomplish my mission."

"What are you talking about, Sarge?" Bart asked.

"The butterfly, Captain. They took the butterfly."

"Who took the butterfly?"

"I never saw them. I think there was more than one. They slugged me from behind and I woke up here and the butterfly was gone. I'm sorry, Captain. The Old Top Sarge let himself get ambushed."

The Negro screamed, "Oh, God! Oh, God-a-mercy, please!"

Across the way the old man murmured, "Martha?"

"Tell me about it, Sarge," urged Bart. "How did you get the butterfly to begin with?"

The Old Sarge looked puzzled. He said, "Why I got it the way you told me to. I went up to Mr. Land's house and he gave me the butterfly, that's all."

"Why did you go to Land's house for the butterfly?"

"Why, because you told me to. At least that old man, that old Jim Lennox that you call your secretary, he called me up in the middle of the night. I was sitting in my room handicapping the sixth at Narragansett and the hall phone rang. It was about two-thirty, almost, anyway, I guess. The phone's

78

right outside my door. So I answered it and the man asked for me and I told him it was me and he said he was James Lennox, Mr. Hardin's secretary, and he said you wanted me to go up to Mr. Land's house right away and do an errand. He said to tell Mr. Land to send you the picture of the butterfly. It sounded screwy, but I didn't ask any questions. He said I was to get the picture of the butterfly and take it to you at your flat right away. So I went. Mr. Land and some young lady was in the house. They'd just come in a few minutes before, he said. Mr. Land had been nibbling at the old juice, because he was kind of tight. He said you must be crazy to send me there for a picture of a butterfly in the middle of the night. But he said it belonged to you and you were welcome to it. He found it laying on a chair, all wrapped up. He opened it up to make sure it was the butterfly, then he wrapped it up again and he handed it to me and said, 'Tell Hardin I know a good psychiatrist if he needs one.' I don't know what he meant by that. He didn't seem to want me to hang around and neither did the young lady, so I went right out and I hadn't walked half a block before something hit me on the head and the next I knew I was here and they told me I didn't have any picture of a butterfly when the cops found me."

"Are you sure it was old Jim Lennox who called you, Sarge?" Bart asked.

"I thought it was. He said it was. He said it was your secretary calling and you wanted me to do an errand. I didn't ask no questions."

Bart nodded. O'Grady didn't know Lennox well enough to recognize his voice on the phone, he thought. And the old soldier would unquestioningly undertake any task he believed Bart has assigned him. The Old Sarge never reasoned why.

O'Grady reared up in bed to a sitting position.

"Captain, did somebody make a patsy out of the Old Top Sarge?" he asked.

Bart patted his hand. "No, Sarge," he replied. "Somebody made a patsy out of Hardin. Somebody started making a patsy out of Hardin about two months ago, in September, to be exact, when they invited him to a card game."

A nurse's aid was passing out breakfast trays. She said to Bart, "You shouldn't stay too long, sir." To O'Grady she said, "You can't have anything but juice until the doctors see you again."

Bart rose. "Is there anything I can get you, Sarge?" he asked. "Anything I can do for you? You're going to be here a few days, they tell me."

"Try to see Moe Selig and ask him to keep my job as lookout for the book," the Sarge said anxiously. "I can't afford to lose that job, Captain."

"I expect Selig already knows about this," Bart said bitterly, "but I'll see him. Anything else?"

"They took the Medal of Honor from around my neck when I come in," the Old Sarge said. "Will you ask 'em to give it back to me?"

"I'll see they do," Bart promised.

Hardin went to the office of the hospital. He deposited money with a cashier, arranged for O'Grady to be moved to a private room. He also arranged that the Old Sarge should get his Medal of Honor back from the property clerk. He called the answering service of a doctor he knew and asked that he drop by the hospital later in the day and attend the Sarge and that the bill be sent to Bart Hardin.

He went out to the street and found a lunchroom and drank three cups of black coffee. He looked at his watch. It was after seven o'clock. He was dead on his feet, but he called a cab and gave the driver the address of the theatrical rooming house on Fifty-third Street where old Jim Lennox resided. The Negro maid was already on duty, dusting and sweeping the halls, when Bart arrived. She knew Hardin and told him he could go to Lennox's room.

"That old man gets up with the birds," she declared. "He's up and dressed every morning when I get here and I get here at seven prompt."

Bart found Lennox in his little room, drinking coffee he had made on an electric plate and eating sweet rolls from a bag while he read a copy of Variety. Lennox told Hardin he knew nothing of the butterfly and had certainly not called the Old Sarge in the middle of the night. Hardin nodded, and left the perplexed old man, refusing to remain for rolls and coffee.

He found another cab and gave the hackie the number of Marty Land's house.

Marty's man Bailey had apparently returned home at a late hour of the morning himself. It was a long while before he opened the door. When he did he was only half dressed. He wore house slippers and trousers and a robe was thrown over his pajama tops. Bailey evidently had adjusted his hours to those of his employer, who was a notorious night owl, Bart thought.

The sleepy-eyed Bailey looked at Bart in astonishment. "Oh, Mr. Hardin!" he exclaimed. "You are abroad at an early hour."

Bart walked through the door although Bailey had made an indecisive gesture of deterring him. "I have to see Mr. Land right away," he said.

Bailey was horrified. "Why, Mr. Hardin!" he said. "I couldn't possibly call Mr. Land at such an hour!" He glanced slyly at a woman's evening cape that had been thrown over a chair in the hall. "Especially this morning," he added.

Bart said, "I'm sorry, Bailey, but it's urgent. You'll have to tell him that I want to see him. If you want to be discreet maybe you could call him on the phone. He keeps one beside his bed for emergencies, I believe."

Bailey bit his lip and rubbed at sleepy eyes. "Really, sir, I don't know what to do. . . ."

Bart strode toward the living room that was still darkened by the drawn draperies. "Call him," he said over his shoulder. He flicked on lights and pulled the drawstrings of the draperies. Bailey went off, muttering to himself. Murky morning light came wanly through the big windows. Bart noted that cigarettes smudged with lipstick were in the ash trays and a highball glass on the table was also red-rimmed.

Bailey returned to the room presently and began to clean up the glasses and the overflowing ash trays. He said, "He'll be down presently, Mr. Hardin. I do hope you will explain that this was urgent. I have strict orders not to call him for any reason before ten."

Bart said, "I'll explain, Bailey."

He had a long wait. Marty finally came in wearing pajamas and a handsome heavy-silk robe. His eyes were bleary and the marks of hangover had drawn his thin, acute face. His chin was bristly and Bart noted that Marty's beard was gray despite the jet-black mustache. He wondered if Marty dyed the mustache.

"You're becoming a real zany character, Hardin," Marty said irritably. "First you send your boy here for a butterfly around three o'clock in the morning and then you wake me up at an hour when no self-respecting rooster should be crowing. I gave the Sarge the name of a good psychiatrist. Why don't you consult him?"

"I tried to reach you all last night, Marty," Bart said. "I left a message for you at eleven different spots. I called here half a dozen times."

"Bailey!" Marty bellowed. "Coffee! Lots of coffee!" He turned to Hardin. "I wasn't in any of the spots you would have called," he said. "I followed Romano down to Twentieth Street in order to protect the interests of my client, Joe Merusi. Joe didn't need me. The D.A. had been tipped that Romano was taking him in. He had Saltus there. Saltus was apparently scared to death that Romano was going to use a rubber hose or something on Joe and we were out of there so fast I could barely get a crossword puzzle started. Since I was so far downtown anyway, I decided to go to a new club in the Village. A young lady who's a protégée of mine is singing there. The proprietor let her off some time around two as a special favor to me. She wanted to come up and see my etchings." Marty leered at Bart. "This young lady is very fond of etchings. It's kind of a bond between us."

Bailey had evidently anticipated his employer's needs and had put coffee on before Marty ordered it. He appeared with a handsome steaming percolator and two cups.

Marty said, "You want an Irish coffee? I've got your brand of bug juice if you do. Or do you still stick to that rule about not taking a drink till four o'clock?"

"It's about the only rule I follow," Bart replied.

"Seems to me to be a bit arbitrary," Marty said. "Personally, I take a drink when I feel like one. I always feel like one when some damn fool wakes me up in the middle of the night." He poured a large portion of brandy into his coffee. "Coffee royal," he said. "God's gift to the dissolute."

He drank from the steaming mixture, smacked his lips. "What gives about this Goddamn butterfly?" he asked. "The young lady and I had been here just about long enough to get some soft music on the recording machine when your emissary barged in. I love the Old Sarge dearly, but at that moment I could have cheerfully split his head."

"Somebody *did* split his head," Bart said.

"What?" asked Marty.

"Some goons jumped the Sarge, right after he left your house, apparently. They broke his head and stole the butterfly. He's down at City now with his head swathed like a swami's."

"But why?" asked Marty. "Why in hell would anybody want the butterfly? Are you trying to tell me that Benny's paintings have suddenly attained a posthumous value? The poor boy had a hard time giving them away when he was alive."

"Somebody called the Sarge and told him he was old Lennox and that I wanted him to come up here and get the butterfly," Bart answered. "Oh, it's got value, Marty. I don't know why, but it has. Joe the Whistler offered me twenty grand for it right after Romano let him loose. Two goons in false faces put a gun on me while they looked for it. Stephanie Breck made an even more attractive offer. Herself."

Hardin told Land the detailed story of the hectic butterfly chase of the previous evening.

Land shook his head. "In my business," he said, "the unexpected is the usual. But this is about the screwiest situation I've encountered in nearly a quarter of a century of practice as the Broadway Mouth."

"There's one thing I can't understand," Bart said. "After I left Stephanie, around three-thirty, I guess it was, I called your house. That was after the Sarge's visit. You must have been here. I guess you were too preoccupied to answer the phone."

"No," Marty replied. "I would have answered if I'd been here. One of the advantages of dealing with the Broadway Mouth is that he offers twenty-four-hour service, like an all-night garage. Most of my clients are the type who get in their worst jams in the middle of the night, in fact. The truth is that my young lady is like most young ladies. She's artistic, but she still prefers food to etchings. She got hungry. Bailey had neglected to leave anything edible on the premises, so after the Sarge left we went around the corner to Reuben's and had some scrambled eggs."

Bart said, "Marty, why the hell did they want the butterfly? Benny told us his brother wanted to destroy it. Romano said there was something about a butterfly he couldn't remember. What's it all about?"

Marty shook his head. He seemed completely bewildered. He drank the rest of his coffee royal. It seemed to restore his good humor. His eyes were twinkling and he smiled at Bart.

"Hardin," he said. "I think I'd like to show you my etchings."

Bart grinned. "Marty," he replied, "this is so sudden."

Marty rose, nodded his head in the direction of his study, said, "Come on."

The study was a small room comfortably furnished in English oak and leather. Several etchings hung above the half-paneling of the walls. Marty pointed to one over the heavy desk. "This is the prize of my collection," he said. "A Whistler, an original impression from the stone. Not a Whistler's Brother, mind you. A real Whistler. A James Abbott McNeill Whistler. Take a look at it. It's exquisite."

Bart peered at the etching. It was a misty river scene, with little boats and barely discernible human figures that seemed to be floating in a fog.

"It's called 'Morning on the Thames,'" Marty said. He placed a finger on the lower right-hand edge of the picture. "Look here. You know what this little design is?"

Bart shrugged. "A kind of curlicue," he said.

"It's a butterfly," Marty replied. "That's the way the original Whistler signed all his work. With that little butterfly design."

Bart stared at Marty. "You think it means something?" he asked.

Marty laughed. "Not a damn thing," he answered. "It couldn't possibly. It doesn't mean anything, but it proves something. It proves you can find a kind of pattern in anything if you look hard enough. That's why so many people believe in astrology and fortune-telling. That's why so many gamblers play hunches."

They left the study and returned to the big living room.

"What about Romano, Marty?" Bart asked.

Marty poured more coffee and brandy for himself and more plain coffee for Hardin. "Not good," he answered. "The D.A.'s office got caught with its pants down, so they're trying to make the police the goat. District attorneys get elected. Homicide lieutenants don't. So it's easier to blame it on the cops, especially on one cop named Romano. Saltus was practically scraping his nose on the floor to me and even to Joe the Whistler last night. It made me kind of sick. I was willing enough for Romano to ask Joe a few questions. Saltus was so panicky he didn't even want that. Saltus told me that Romano was in bad for not putting through a routine report to the D.A. before he put the collar on the Whistler last night. He indicated Romano's got another date with Commissioner tomorrow afternoon. If he doesn't do anything foolish between now and then, maybe he's all right. But it's not good, it's not good at all, Hardin."

Bart said, "I wish to God he could remember what it is that he forgot about the butterfly."

Marty shrugged. "I think we've all got butterflies in the

belfry," he said. "Take me. For once in my life, I've got the
D.A.'s office right where I want it. Broderick and Saltus
pulled such a boo-boo when they put that witness on the
stand that they're back-pedaling with all four feet. They'd
hand me City Hall tied up in pink ribbon if I asked for it.
They're practically acting as counsel for my client because of
what they almost did to him with that perjured witness. It's
a criminal lawyer's dream. And I don't like it. I hate to see
any man made into a fall-guy. Especially if he's a man like
Romano. Probably Romano doesn't really have anything to
remember about a butterfly. It may be just some vague and
meaningless association of ideas, some frantic seeking for a
pattern. The kind of thing I demonstrated when I showed
you Whistler's butterfly signature. Romano doesn't often
forget anything important. His mind is like a trap. Or maybe
he's just slipping, I don't know."

Hardin finished his coffee and got to his feet. Five cups of
coffee and innumerable cigarettes before breakfast had made
his stomach queasy. He needed food.

Bart said, "I don't think Romano's slipping. I think Romano's just plain mad."

"Public servants and especially cops can't afford the luxury
of getting mad," said Marty. "They have to do the hardest
thing that any man is asked to do. They have to stay ob-
jective."

Marty followed Bart into the hall. "I'm going back to bed,"
he said. "I'm a growing boy and I need my beauty sleep."

Hardin looked significantly at the woman's evening wrap
that was thrown upon the chair. He grinned at Land. "Sleep
tight, Marty," he said.

It was eight o'clock. The cold November morning light was
steady in the streets now and people were abroad in increasing numbers, moving as city-dwellers always seem to move at
this early hour, in a kind of frantic daze. Hardin shivered and
buttoned his trenchcoat up around his neck. There was winter
in the wind. He found a cab and rode to the Copper Skillet, a
Broadway restaurant that specialized in ham and eggs, where
he almost always ate his breakfast. Usually, however, he did
not eat it until noon, and his appearance caused comment on
the part of the cashier and the waitress. The ham and eggs and
several slabs of buttered toast and yet another cup of coffee
restored his vitality to some extent. He walked down Broadway toward the flea circus, hoping he could get an hour or
two of sleep before his duties at the Broadway Times began.

Broadway, he thought, was a dismal place at this hour of the morning. Most of its lights still glimmered through the smoky autumn haze. From a signboard a man with a forty-foot head blew real smoke through a hole that was ten feet wide to advertise a brand of cigarettes. The streets themselves were almost deserted except for the lines that were forming before picture palaces which charged one-third of their regular prices to those who arrived by nine-thirty in the morning. A crew of despondent-looking sanitation workers shoved push-brooms and piled up the Big Street's rubbish that split into separate parts and renewed itself perpetually like some primitive one-cell organism. The tempo of the Street would increase as afternoon approached, but on Broadway day did not begin until it was night.

When he was in his flat, Bart looked at his possessions that the men in rubber masks had piled as casually as the street cleaners piled the rubbish. He decided the task of cleaning up was too much for him. He would leave extra money for the maid who was due today to do the job instead. He took another shower, hoping the tepid water would relax him and bring sleep. He stretched out naked on the bed, but he found he was far too tense to drift off into sleep. The half-dozen coffees had hardly helped, either.

His good deed, he thought bitterly, had brought misfortune to yet another innocent victim. Because of his testimony, Romano's long career might be ended under a cloud. A bumbling, addled youth who painted pictures with his fingers was dead. And now Eddie O'Grady, the Top Sarge, an old man who had been eager to render him a small favor, lay in a hospital with a broken head.

Never join the Boy Scouts, Bart told himself.

A sleep of sorts came finally, but it was troubled sleep. He dreamed that he was fighting off a swarm of butterflies. The butterflies had multi-colored wings that glistened like stained glass, like the wings of the butterfly that Benny Merusi had painted.

Once again it was the phone that awakened him.

When he answered he was surprised to hear the grating, mocking voice of Moe Selig, the bookmaker and loan shark, the Syndicate lieutenant who was called the Great Pawnbroker of Broadway.

Hardin said, "I was going to call you, although I don't think there's much use. You probably know already that the

Old Sarge had an accident and can't get to work for several days."

"I know," said Selig with mock concern. "I heard the rumble, Hardin. I'm going to send him a big good-luck wreath to the hospital. The Sarge will like that, don't you think? Now, who do you suppose would want to hurt that poor old man?"

Hardin could imagine Selig's silent laughter as he said that.

"If you see the Sarge, you tell him Selig will hold his job open, Hardin. You tell him Selig always takes care of the boys. What I called about is I want you to do me a big favor if you will. I want you should stop by here on your way to work. I got a little matter to take up."

"What?" asked Hardin.

Selig could not keep the mirth out of his voice when he replied. "You'll see, Hardin!" he promised. "It's something real nice!"

nine

It was nearing noon when a haggard Hardin walked down Jacobs Beach toward Moe Selig's horse room. He was uncomfortably conscious of the attention he was attracting from the punters and managers and runners and touts and hangers-on who were assembled on the Beach for the usual midday ceremonies of exchanging gossip and tips and opinions regarding the all-important subjects of horseraces to be run at the tracks that afternoon and prizefights to be decided at the Garden that evening. They didn't greet him, but a silence fell over each little group as he approached and faces lit up briefly with sly, quick smiles. Hardin was aware that the loungers began to whisper among themselves as soon as he had passed. He felt that somehow, in a way he could not explain, he was the butt of some huge joke.

Moe Selig prided himself on a sense of humor.

Usually the victims of Selig's jokes were the helpless stumblebums of Broadway.

Hardin wondered if Selig, who had always shown him a grudging respect, had suddenly decided he belonged in the ranks of the stumblebums.

He entered the smoke shop. A slim young man with a dark and evil face was sitting in the Old Sarge's usual place behind the cigar counter. He was digging at his fingernails with a penknife. Hardin recognized him as one of the innumerable drifters who seemed to serve some vague function in Selig's little empire, by just hanging around the fringes if nothing else, but he didn't even know the hoodlum's name. The young man grinned insultingly at Hardin as if he were some peculiarly interesting specimen impaled upon a pin. He continued to stare at Hardin and to clean his fingernails.

Hardin nodded toward the heavy door of the horse room

in the rear. "I want to see Selig," he said curtly. "Get off your tail and open the door."

The slim young hood arose with mock courtesy. "Why, of course, *Mister* Hardin," he said. "Moe Selig says to tell you you're welcome here any time. You rate aces with the boss, Mister Hardin."

The lookout walked to the door and pressed a buzzer. When it was opened he said, "*Mister* Hardin's here. He wants to see the boss."

He made a little ceremony of conducting Hardin through the horse room. Sheet-writers, cashiers, block men were setting up for business. They regarded Hardin with surreptitious amusement as he walked toward Selig's office with the mockingly obsequious young man acting as his guard of honor. The young man knocked on Selig's door. A buzzer released the lock and the lookout pushed the door open. He stood aside and made a sweeping gesture to indicate that Hardin should enter.

Selig sat behind his big desk in his shirtsleeves. He was a man of sixty, short of stature but very wide in the shoulders and long of arm. He had the hunched, deformed appearance of a middle-sized ape. His thin, pasty face had a wrinkled, alert and slightly simian look, too. He grinned widely as Hardin entered and gold teeth glittered in his mouth. "Hello, editor!" he exclaimed. "You're a real pal to come see Selig. A real pal, that's what you are."

On the desk beside Selig was a large package, gift-wrapped. The gambling boss was drinking a cup of coffee. Also on the desk was a large cardboard coffee container. Steam was still rising from it.

"Sit down, chum, sit right down," Selig said. "Have a cup of coffee with me. If you want a drink of hard stuff, I got that, too."

Hardin said, "No, thanks."

He sat down in a chair beside the desk without removing his hat.

"I tell you why I asked you here, editor," Selig said. "The boys wanted to do something for you. The boys are mighty happy about what you did for Joe the Whistler yesterday and they want to show you their appreciation. Some of the boys are rough around the edges, maybe, but when they find out you're a pal, the sky's the limit with them. Only trouble is the boys are kind of crude. One of them suggested we should fix a fight at the Garden tonight and let you bet on the guy that we

elect. Another one thought we should fix you up for free with
a hundred-dollar call girl. But I said no. The boys mean well,
but they don't understand. This Hardin's a gentleman, I told
them. He's a real important man, a editor. Anything you do
for Hardin has got to be refined, I said."

Bart waited.

Selig drank more coffee, leaned back in his chair. The grin
was spread all over his crinkled monkey's face. He said, "So
the boys said they'd leave the whole thing to Selig. I said to
them, Look, boys, this Hardin's a real gentleman, like those
characters in the liquor ads with their guns and bird dogs.
Gentlemen have got hobbies. You take this Hardin, now. His
hobby is butterflies. If you were going to give Ike Eisenhower
a present, I told them, you'd give him a golf club on account
of golf's his hobby. Hardin's the same way about butterflies
that Ike is about golf."

Selig paused again and leaned back in the chair. He was
always circuitous and he was enjoying himself so much he
wanted to draw it out.

"We got to give Hardin some present that's got something
to do with his hobby, I told them," Selig continued. "Now if
he was a fisherman, we could give him a rod and reel, but who
the hell can fish on Jacobs Beach? Believe me, pal, I thought
it over. I thought real hard. The boys took up a collection
and gave me some money to buy a present for you. One of the
boys thought we should buy you a butterfly net because you
like butterflies so much, but, tell you the truth, I don't know
where the hell you buy butterfly nets because personally I
never had any occasion to use one. But this morning I got up
early and went shopping. I went to a real fancy shop on
Broadway and I found just the thing for you."

Selig rose ceremoniously from his chair, picked up the gift-
wrapped box and handed it to Hardin. "With the compli-
ments of the boys, Hardin," he said. "They all chipped in to
buy it because you're a real pal."

Selig sat down again, shaking with silent laughter.

There wasn't anything to do but open it, Bart decided. He
ripped off the wrapping and threw it on Selig's floor. The box
bore the label of a Broadway haberdasher who appealed to
the somewhat flamboyant tastes of the Garden sports crowd.
Hardin opened the box.

Inside was a fancy vest, far gaudier than any of those in his
own rather extensive collection. It was made of heavy satin

and it was intricately embroidered with an over-all design of multi-colored butterflies.

"Ain't it nice, chum?" Selig asked happily. "Just the thing for you. You like trick vests and you like butterflies and now you got both."

Hardin stood up and tossed the vest across the desk to Selig. He said, "It should come in handy. You can wipe your face with it."

The grin disappeared from Selig's face. His eyes were narrowed and his expression wary. He said, his voice uncertain, "My face ain't wet, chum."

Hardin picked up the cardboard coffee container. He hurled the contents into Selig's face.

He said, "Now it's wet, Selig."

The coffee wasn't scalding but it was hot. Selig winced as the brown liquid splashed full into his face. Then for a long moment he sat tense, silent, as if he were about to spring. The coffee had cream in it. The cream hung in little clotted curds from Selig's thick eyebrows and made chalky beads on his eyelashes. The coffee dripped down from his face onto his white-on-white shirt and the stain crept over the floral hand-painted tie he was wearing. Selig did not raise a hand to wipe off the liquid even though the sting of it had brought tears into his eyes. He just sat and stared at Hardin. A full minute passed before he reached into a drawer and very slowly drew out a towel. Still deliberate and still completely silent, Selig began to dry his face, to pat at his shirt and tie. Hardin stood and waited.

Selig looked at his ruined tie. He seemed detached and contemplative. He said, "You loused up my tie, chum. Joe the Whistler gave me that tie. There's a guy who makes them, just one of a kind. They cost a double-saw apiece."

When Selig had finally wiped away the worst of the sticky mess, he put the towel back in the drawer, soaking wet as it was. He said, "You know what's under the towel in the drawer, chum? A gun. A forty-five that makes a big, fat hole. Fifteen or twenty years ago, you'd be dead now if you'd done that to Selig, chum. You'd be down there on the carpet with blood all over you. Or maybe I would have saved you for the boys. The boys could have a lot of fun, doing it to you real slow. By tonight you'd be all dressed up in a cement overcoat so you'd sink real quick when they dropped you in the river with the other garbage. But not now. The organization don't work like that now. The organization is big business, like Standard Oil. Don't worry about a thing, chum. I ain't going to kill you. I ain't even going to have the muscle boys work you over and break some bones for what you did to Selig."

Selig closed his eyes that were still leaking tears from the sting of the hot liquid. He spoke slowly. "All I'm going to do is run you off Broadway, Hardin. I'm going to fix it so you couldn't get a job cleaning out the can of a cheap saloon. I'll tell you how I'm going to do it, chum. The organization owns a lot of theatres and night spots and it puts money into a lot of Broadway shows. Those theatres and shows and night spots advertise in your blat, the *Broadway Times*. Or they did up until today. After today, they don't. Neither do a lot of bars and restaurants where Selig's got some influence. Selig is going to see that Maddox Slade, who owns your blat, knows why his advertising is falling off. He's going to know it's falling off because people don't like Hardin any more. Selig is going to do something else, too. He's going to start a rumble around the Street. The rumble is going to be that the Whistler paid you off in big coarse notes last night in the Sligo Slasher's bar for what you did for him. When Selig starts a rumble it gets heard around. Maddox Slade is going to hear it. And Billy Beecher who writes that Broadway gossip column in the tabs is going to print it. Selig can see to that. It can't hurt Joe the Whistler any, not now it can't. They can't try him for chilling Breck again. They can't try him for anything or put the heat on anybody, because the butterfly is gone."

Selig opened his eyes. Curded coffee cream still stuck to the rims of the eyelids like mucus.

"Goodbye, Hardin," Selig said, "It was nice of you to come."

Hardin said, "So long, Selig. And thanks for everything."

He turned his back on Selig, walked toward the door, opened it. The slim young hood was just outside. He was still digging at his fingernails with a penknife. There was an expectant grin on his face. He glanced into the office and saw the disheveled Selig. A look of alarm came into his face. He moved in front of Hardin as if to block him.

"Is something wrong, boss?" he asked.

Hardin thrust a bill into the hood's hand. "Selig spilt his coffee," he said. "Run out and get him some more."

Hardin thrust the young hood roughly out of his way. He walked rapidly through the horse room, through the smoke shop, out into the street.

Idlers had gathered in small groups just outside the smoke shop, obviously to await the result of Selig's little joke. Bart pushed through them. One or two men spoke to him tentatively, asked him about the butterfly vest. Hardin didn't answer. He walked to Eighth Avenue, turned uptown. He crossed the street at Fifty-first and entered the office of the *Broadway Times*.

As he strode through the city room he noted with some surprise that Mrs. Phoebe Barclay Washburn was honoring the office with one of her infrequent visits. Mrs. Phoebe Barclay Washburn was a plump, corseted and gray-haired lady who possessed an abundance of social prestige and very little money. She owned a foreign car driven by a uniformed chauffeur, she lived on the fashionable East Side, she patronized the more elegant dressmakers, she lunched regularly at the Colony and she lived largely by her wits. She was a protégée of Maddox Slade. He had engaged her as a columnist in the hope that she could serve him more privately in furthering his social ambitions, which were considerable. Mrs. Phoebe Barclay Washburn wrote a snobbish column of chit-chat called "Café Society" for the *Broadway Times* under the name of "Penelope Peabody." Bart had seldom spoken to her and, although he was managing editor of the paper, he had never yet read one of her columns. Mrs. Washburn usually wrote her columns at home and had them delivered by her chauffeur. Today she sat at a battered typewriter in the old city room, pecking disdainfully with two fingers. She was elegantly gowned and severely girdled and she wore a hat on her regally empurpled coiffure that reminded Bart of an inverted waste can embellished with artichokes. The spectacle of this doughty dowager pounding a typewriter alongside shirtsleeved racetrack selectors, prizefight columnists and Broadway reporters was almost too much for Hardin. He could hardly keep himself from breaking into laughter.

Bart stopped beside the lady's desk. He said, "How do you do, Mrs. Washburn? I wonder if you'd step into my office a minute when you have time?"

Mrs. Washburn looked up. "Well, Mr. Hardin!" she said. "I'm flattered. In all the years I've been working for the paper this is the first time our managing editor has deigned to notice me. I'll come right now."

She followed Bart into the cubbyhole that was already occupied by old Jim Lennox. Jim had straightened up the usual mess on Bart's desk as best he could. He had sharpened all the pencils. He had slit open the morning mail and arranged it in what he thought was the proper order of importance. Now Bart had to find something else for him to do. One of his larger problems was finding things for Lennox to do, so the old man would not feel that the weekly stipend Bart paid him was charity.

Hardin said, "Mrs. Washburn, this is my secretary, Mr. James Lennox."

Mrs. Washburn smiled graciously and extended a small, pudgy and bejeweled hand to Lennox. "I feel we're old friends," she said. "I saw you on the stage many times, Mr. Lennox. I especially remember your performance in *Dear Brutus*. That rather dates me, doesn't it?"

Lennox took her hand and gave Mrs. Washburn a courtly bow. "Thank you, dear lady," he said. "Thank you for remembering me."

"Jim, I'm planning some Sunday features on old-time Broadway gamblers," Bart said. "Go back to the morgue and see what pictures and clips you can dig up on Richard Canfield, will you?"

"Certainly, Bart, certainly," the old man said happily. He gave Mrs. Washburn another courtly bow and left.

Mrs. Washburn sat down. She looked curiously at the pictures of racehorses and semi-nude chorus girls that had been tacked to the beaverboard walls of the office. She said, "Well, Mr. Hardin, you have quite an art gallery." She discovered the fingerpainting of a horse in motion that Benny Merusi had presented to Bart. She rose and examined it. "It's odd to find this here," she said. "It's an original, isn't it? A very interesting abstraction. The painter must have had a most unusual imagination."

"I suppose so," Bart answered. "It was painted by a mentally retarded boy."

Mrs. Washburn seated herself again and laughed. "I'm rather afraid I consider all modernists to be mentally retarded," she said. "I'm a rather stuffy old thing, I suppose. I still like Gainsboroughs and antimacassars and fish forks with the fish course."

"Mrs. Washburn, I need some information," Bart said. "I'd like for you to tell me everything you know about Stephanie Breck, the widow of Jason Breck."

Mrs. Washburn smiled brightly. "Personally interested, Mr. Hardin? I can't blame you. She's very beautiful and now her husband has departed this vale of tears she's also immensely rich. She's trash, of course. But when trash comes in such a delectable mold as Stephanie it is accepted by present-day society as a delicacy. I am referring to one of the more obnoxious phenomena of our time, café society, of course. It seems incredible, but it is now quite possible for some curvaceous tramp from Hollywood who has no more breeding than an alley cat to move in the same circles with people of family. I fancy that's why my poor column has some value to dear Maddox who owns a Broadway paper. Hollywood and Broadway rub elbows with people of breeding in the only remaining gathering places of New York society, the cafés. If it weren't so shockingly horrible to a person of sensitivity, it would seem ludicrous. The most important social arbiters we have today are these gangster persons of foreign extraction who own cafés. It's their arbitrary table seatings at their clubs and restaurants that counts now, not the family tree. Shades of dear Ward MacAllister and the Four Hundred!"

"I'd like to know something a bit more personal about Stephanie Breck," Bart interrupted her.

"Of course!" exclaimed Mrs. Washburn. "There I go wandering again. But dear Maddox says that's part of the charm of my column, the way I wander. Stephanie Breck was born in Brooklyn. She's supposed to be Hungarian, but her father was a bartender with some Irish name, Casey, I think. She was a pretty trollop clerking behind a perfume counter when some independent movie producer became infatuated with her and took her to Hollywood. He made a film with her in it and her figure became famous overnight. She left her benefactor flat and went to one of the big studios. She had several sordid affairs with nasty little men like singing cowboys and prizefighters and then Jason Breck found her and married her and brought her to New York. Jason Breck was not society, but he was a man I rather liked. He had money and in New York society, money is power and he forced the acceptance of his bride in the best circles. She treated him outrageously by flaunting her lovers in his face, but he wouldn't throw her out. She is a completely unacceptable person under any of the ordinary standards of polite society. Yet she was accepted, almost without question, because she was considered to possess the dubious quality called glamour and she was the wife of a rich man named Jason Breck. Even I accepted her in a sense. I didn't invite her to my home, of course, but I didn't snub her. I have always thought the mark of a gentlewoman is her courtesy toward all classes. Besides, I have learned to adjust. I've had to."

"That's all you know about her?" Hardin asked.

Mrs. Washburn said, "There is one thing to her credit. She has an interesting, though rather expensive, hobby. She collects historic jewelry. Not just jewels—jewelry. She owns pieces that have decorated the great women of the past and they are in their original settings. The Empress Josephine tiara, the ear-drops that Pompadour wore, have a value far beyond their intrinsic worth."

Mrs. Washburn thought a minute. She said, "I'm afraid that's about all I can tell you. I can understand her attraction for men. I'm realistic enough for that. They're more civilized about such things in France. In France a gentleman of substance would keep such a woman. He wouldn't marry her."

"Can you think of any reason why a butterfly or a picture of a butterfly should be connected with Stephanie Breck?" Bart asked.

"A butterfly? What an extraordinary question, Mr. Hardin! I suppose there might be some connection if you used the old cliché and compared her to a butterfly. That seems to be a fairly standard term for loose, immoral women. Personally, I have always thought the butterfly was a much maligned insect. I suppose that from the entomological viewpoint, the sex life of the butterfly may be peculiar, but I really doubt that lady butterflies are as promiscuous as Stephanie Breck and her kind."

Mrs. Washburn shook her head. "Really! Butterflies!" she exclaimed. "What a very odd topic for conversation. You know, I don't believe I've ever in my life discussed butterflies with anyone before."

Bart thought, I've learned absolutely nothing, but of course I was playing a hunch, a longshot, anyway. He said, "Thank you very much, Mrs. Washburn. I won't keep you away from your work any longer."

Mrs. Washburn said, "Well, it's been—interesting. Although I must confess I don't know what it's all about. Mr. Hardin, I do wish you would tell dear Maddox to buy some decent typewriters for this place. My poor little portable broke down and I had to send it in for repairs. That machine in the city room should be used for threshing wheat."

Mrs. Washburn rose. She bestowed a gracious smile on Bart and left the little office.

There might be clippings in the morgue that would cast further light on Stephanie Breck, but Bart doubted it. Most of them would refer to her movie career and would be largely drawn from the fables of Hollywood press agents. The others would deal with her social activities as the wife of Jason Breck, and doubtless Mrs. Washburn in her role of "Penelope Peabody" had written them. Bart thought he might set old Jim Lennox the task of searching for a butterfly among Mrs. Breck's press notices. At least it would serve the purpose of giving Jim something else to do.

There was no reason to believe that the butterfly was connected with Stephanie at all, of course, other than her effort to obtain it. She might have tried to obtain it solely because she seemed to be completely under the influence of Joe the Whistler, who also had wanted the butterfly. The butterfly might well be connected with the Whistler himself, or with the Whistler's brother, or with the murdered Jason Breck.

Hardin thought of what Mrs. Washburn had said about the mobsters who owned cafés being the real arbiters of modern society. It was a remarkably acute observation and it was unquestionably true. Men who had once been rum-runners, procurers and bouncers in speakeasies ruled New York society with a velvet rope. A man's social standing was determined largely by the table he occupied in a café society resort and the table was assigned or withheld according to the whim of a goon in a dinner jacket who could barely read and write.

This incredible fact was an amusing byproduct of the mob's increasing omnipotence. But the Syndicate's omnipotence wasn't really funny. Its almost unopposed power in nearly every phase of human endeavor was downright frightening. Its estimated national income of twenty billion dollars a year from illegal gambling alone was just about twice the gross income of the entire automotive industry.

Moe Selig was one of the Syndicate's gambling czars and Moe Selig had threatened to run Bart Hardin right off Broadway.

Hardin had to face the simple, bitter truth.

It was entirely possible that Moe Selig could do exactly what he had threatened he would do.

Old Lennox returned from the morgue carrying stuffed envelopes and yellowed clippings. He sat down at a little table Bart had placed in the office to serve as his desk and began to sort the clippings. He said, "There's some fascinating material on Dick Canfield here. He was a type who's disappeared

completely from the Broadway scene. A gentleman gambler.
Did you know that Whistler painted a famous portrait of
him? It was a kind of joke. He had Canfield pose in clerical
robes and called the portrait 'His Reverence.' "

"Please, Jim," Bart said. "I'd rather not hear any more
about paintings or people called Whistler today."

The old man's brows knit with perplexity. "What, Bart?"
he asked.

"Skip it, Jim," Bart said.

"Would you like me to write out a little précis of the
material on Canfield?" the old man asked.

Bart smiled. He thought, Some day I might actually run a
Sunday feature on old-time Broadway gamblers. Meanwhile
the project would keep Jim happily occupied.

"You do that, Jim," he said. "And when you finish I've got
another job for you. I want you to go back to the morgue
and see what clippings we have on . . ."

He was interrupted by the ringing of the telephone.

He picked up the phone and Marty Land answered.

"If you can tear yourself away from your work, editor, I
think you should drop around here," Land said. "There have
been some very interesting developments in the past hour or
so. I think you'd like to know about them."

"What developments?" Bart asked.

"For one thing, I've just made Selig mad as hell. I've
refused to take a case he offered me. You'd better drop
around. It shouldn't take too long."

Bart said, "I'll be right over."

He hung up the phone.

"What was the other job you had for me, Bart?" Lennox
asked.

"Never mind it now," said Bart. "Stick to Canfield. I have
to go out for about an hour. Hold down the fort till I get
back."

"Where will I say you are if there's a call?" the old man
asked.

Bart was struggling into his coat. He looked over his shoulder at Lennox and said, "Just tell 'em I'm chasing butterflies."

ten

The woman's evening wrap was missing from the chair in Marty's hall when Bart arrived at the house on East Sixtieth.

Bailey ushered Hardin into the living room. Marty had shaved the gray bristles from his face and waxed his mustache. He was comfortably attired in slacks and a cashmere sweater.

"No work today, counselor?" Bart asked.

Marty shook his head. "Never work the day after I've won a case if I can help it," he answered. "Especially the day after I've beaten a murder rap. That's one of the reasons I refused Selig when he called and asked me to act for a certain client. There are other reasons, though."

Bart sat down. Marty yawned and stretched himself expansively. "No rest for Marty this morning," he said. "First the Old Sarge comes here hunting for a butterfly. Then you arrive. A little while ago, when I was finally beginning to rest comfortably, Selig called on the private line. He told me he wanted me to represent a client and he would guarantee the fee. I refused. Selig blew his top. Says he's taking his business away from Marty again. Maybe he will, but he'll be back. Every time Selig takes his business away from Marty, the electricity bills at Sing Sing go up. It could cost me ten thousand, though. I was supposed to get a ten-thousand-dollar bonus if I beat the Whistler's rap. Selig says the Syndicate will see Joe doesn't pay me the bonus he owes me."

"Who was the client?" Bart asked.

"That's the wowser," Marty replied. "The client Selig wished me to represent was Isadore Feldheim. Busy Izzy, the perjured witness."

"What?" said Bart.

Marty nodded. "That's right. Busy Izzy. Yesterday the Syndicate pays me a big, stiff fee to keep one of its boys named

99

Joe the Whistler from burning in the hot squat. In the course
of earning my money I proved Busy Izzy was a perjurer. Today
the Syndicate wants to pay me another big, stiff fee for defending Busy Izzy on the charge I brought against him."

"Did Selig explain why?"

"No," said Marty. "Selig never explains. Selig just orders."

"Do you think the boys want Izzy out of jail so they can
take care of him themselves?" Bart asked.

Marty shrugged his trim, sweatered shoulders. "I've quit
thinking. It makes the hair fall out."

"What did you tell Selig?"

"I told him that under the circumstances the law might
take a very dim view if I appeared as Izzy's counsel. I told him
certain suspicious souls might detect a delicate odor of
fromage in the whole business. Selig didn't think so. He
thought it would add weight to Izzy's plea if the same lawyer
who had been the cause of his trouble were to appear in his
behalf. Besides, he pointed out it would be the easiest retainer that I ever earned. And it would have been. Any kid
fresh out of law school can get Izzy out of durance vile this
afternoon."

"Why?" asked Bart. "I thought my testimony made the
case against him pretty ironclad. Judge Tevis seemed to think
so, too."

Marty said, "Because a couple of people have suddenly
remembered something they forgot. At least, that's what Selig
says."

"What people?"

"Dolly Buffo, the distinguished proprietor of Dolly Buffo's
Grill, is one," Marty replied. "He's a highly reputable citizen
of our city, now that he owns one of its most prosperous
cafés, even though certain evil-minded people seem to suspect
he has Syndicate connections. Izzy has an even better witness, a witness whose name is in the Social Register. Joey
Marsten, the society playboy, who is one of Buffo's regular
patrons."

"What the hell do they remember?" Bart asked.

"They remember that Izzy was telling the absolute truth
when he stated that he picked up Joe the Whistler in front
of Buffo's Grill at two-thirty in the morning," Marty answered.

"But he couldn't have been. He came into that room of
the Mid-City Hotel at two-thirty in the morning."

"Poor Izzy just had his dates mixed a little, it seems,"
said Marty. "He picked up Joe on the morning of September

seventh, not the morning of September eighth when Jason Breck was killed. Dolly Buffo is very sure of the date, because September seventh is his birthday. He had been buying drinks for Marsten at the bar to celebrate the occasion and Joe the Whistler came over and started talking horses with Marsten, who owns a racing stable. Dolly walked out of the café with them to bid them good night. Both Marsten and Buffo know Izzy because he hacks the spot regularly. They saw Izzy come up in his cab and they saw Joe the Whistler get in it."

Marty shook his head. "No grand jury on earth would indict a man for perjury because he got mixed up in re-membering a date. Izzy's case won't even reach a grand jury. All a lawyer has to do is produce the witnesses, explain the thing, and Izzy is out. Still, I didn't think I should be the lawyer in the matter. It could hardly help my professional reputation any if I appeared in Izzy's behalf after the happen-ings of yesterday. It might make me seem decidedly versatile, but hardly ethical, I'm afraid."

"But Joe the Whistler knew this, certainly," Bart said. "If he'd told you, you could have blasted the prosecution's case merely by calling Buffo and Marsten and cross-examining Izzy. Why the hell didn't Joe the Whistler tell you?"

Marty smiled. "In the words of the despondent Dane named Hamlet, that is the question," he said.

"Does it make any sense at all to you, Marty?" Bart asked.

"To Selig it must make sense," Marty said. "I've got to know the estimable Moe rather well over the years. He bears a close resemblance to a bag full of eels. Usually, however, I can follow the somewhat devious machinery of his mind. Usually, I can even anticipate his moves. This time I confess I can't. This time my agile little brain is completely baffled by the Selig strategy."

"I saw Selig today," Bart said. "I threw a container of coffee in his face. Selig says he's going to run me right off Broadway. I think it's possible he can."

Bart told Marty what had happened. "Is there any legal recourse I can take, Marty?" he asked. "Could I get a re-straining order or something against him?"

Marty said, "You can't serve a restraining order on a bag of eels, I'm afraid."

"Selig says he's going to plant a lie in Billy Beecher's column tonight that I was bribed to testify for Joe the Whistler. Is there anything we can do about that?"

"There may be. But not before the item's printed. After

that we can sue for libel. The fact that Buffo and Marsten will say that Izzy testified wrongly as to the date will indicate your own testimony was accurate. That would make a strong case for us if he prints the item. I'd rather like to do something mean to Billy. He's a nasty little man. There's no doubt he'll print the story if Selig tells him to. He toadies to the Syndicate and always has. They feed him tips on crime news occasionally in exchange for him puffing the performers at Syndicate clubs. I wouldn't doubt that he was on Selig's payroll. For an employer who pays no social security, Selig has a rather large payroll."

"After it's printed, it will be too late, I'm afraid," Hardin said. "Maddox Slade will flip his top completely if he sees a story that his managing editor has been bribed by mobsters, whether it's true or not. Slade has made a fortune off a paper that sells past performances and tips on horses and Broadway gossip, but he comes down with a hard case of the shakes if scandal touches him or his property just the same."

"There's not much chance of stopping it," Marty said. "Billy Beecher has got a contract that won't be renewed, I understand, but it hasn't run out yet. It stipulates his copy runs as written, with no censorship whatsoever. Libel suits are a constant annoyance to his paper because of it, but apparently there's nothing they can do about it."

Bart stood up. "Well, I've got at least one more paper to put out," he said. "Thanks for the information. I don't know what it means, but thanks, anyway. Also thanks for the legal advice. Maybe if Selig runs me off Broadway I can open up a chicken farm. That's what Romano has always said he was going to do when he retired. Maybe we could go into partnership."

"Don't open a chicken farm," Marty advised. "When you do anything, do it with a flourish. Open up a peacock farm."

Bart returned to the *Broadway Times*. Old Lennox was awaiting him anxiously.

"I tried to call you at several places I thought you might be," Lennox said. "The composing room skipper wants to see you right away."

Hardin walked through the city room, climbed the rickety flight of stairs to the composing room. He walked through rows of clattering linotypes and waiting type forms to the copy-cutter's desk, where the composing room skipper stood, looking grim. The skipper's name was Folsom and he was a big man with a great belly and salt-and-pepper eyebrows. He glared at Bart.

"We got grief, Hardin," he said.

Composing room skippers never brought tidings of anything but grief, Hardin reflected.

"We got more wide open spaces in the forms than they got in a Western movie," Folsom went on. "I already used up nearly five columns of the overset and we need plenty more filler before we get to press. Advertising has canceled about half the amusement lineage already and they tell me more is coming."

So it's started, Hardin thought.

Moe Selig's campaign had already begun.

Hardin said, "Okay. I'll go down and start copy moving up."

"If I got to put filler on the machines at this time of day, I'll have to keep some operators overtime to get the late race charts out. The front office ain't going to like that," the skipper said darkly.

Hardin had fully expected that it would happen, but he had not expected it to happen so soon. It hardly seemed possible that even an organization of the Syndicate's power could move so quickly. Blanton, the advertising manager, was waiting in Hardin's office when he returned from the composing room.

"Can you explain what's happening, Hardin?" he asked. "There are thirty-one shows running on Broadway at the moment. Fourteen of them have canceled their advertising in the *Broadway Times*. That includes the considerable display advertising we've been running for the hit shows as well as the regular daily twenty-eight-line notices for all of them. And that's not all. Cancellations from clubs and restaurants are coming in faster than we can handle the phone calls! I've tried to find out why. All I can learn is that the orders seem to come from the top. And I've had nasty hints that it's because of something you did. What did you do, Hardin? I've been on this paper eighteen years and nothing like this has ever happened before. It practically amounts to a boycott."

"Who told you it was because of me and what did they say I did?" Bart asked.

"That's just it. There's nothing really definite. I've called the advertising agents and press agents and friends of mine connected with the theatres and clubs to see what's caused this. All I get is sly hints. They tell me to ask our managing editor or they say it's all that Hardin's fault and then they just clam up."

"How much space is going to be canceled?" Hardin asked. "I'll either have to fill it or cut down the size of the paper tonight."

Blanton shook his head helplessly. "It already amounts to thousands of lines," he said. "About two full pages, I'd say. Lord knows how much it will add up to before we're finished."

Hardin said, "I'll try to keep the paper to normal size. I'll try to fill up the holes somehow."

"That may solve your problem," Blanton replied. "It doesn't solve mine. Now we're beginning to get cancellations of sport advertising, even. Not too much yet. We've still got the big accounts like the Garden, but the club arenas all over town, all over the Bronx and Staten Island and Long Island, are dropping off. Filling the holes may be fine for you but it doesn't make up for the thousands we're losing in advertising revenue. I have to call Slade on this, Hardin. He'll have to know. I'll have to tell him about the hints. If you want to make some explanation, I'm listening, or you can call him up yourself."

"Thanks," Bart replied. "There isn't any explanation except that the Syndicate is mad at me. You know as well as I do that the Syndicate has a financial finger in a lot of Broadway theatres and in virtually all of the Broadway clubs in one way or another, even if it doesn't own them outright. The Syndicate can bring pressure if it wants to."

"But I thought you'd be the white-haired boy of the Syndicate after you testified for that bookie yesterday!" Blanton said. "I don't understand."

"A little while ago I heard someone describe Moe Selig as a bag of eels," Hardin answered. "It's pretty hard to guess which way a bag of eels is going to squirm."

Blanton left, shaking his head. He said, "I'm sorry, Hardin. But I'll have to call Slade."

Hardin began to fish in a drawer of his desk. Beneath a bottle of Irish whisky he found stacks of copy Jim Lennox had written, an old actor's reminiscences of a Broadway of a mellower day. He had had Jim do the stories as rainy-day fillers mainly to occupy his time, never dreaming he would find use for them. They had been written in longhand, but fortunately he'd had them typed.

He turned to Lennox and grinned. "Jim," he said, "tonight

you're going to be the most prolific newspaper writer in New York City."

Hardin called the art department and ordered photographs sent for engraving. He called the morgue and had old cuts of famous Broadway figures of another era sent in to illustrate Lennox's numerous stories. He was determined that with or without advertising the paper would run to its usual size that night. He wasn't going to give the boys the satisfaction of seeing a skimpy paper on the stands. He told old Pops Taylor, the racing editor, to send up all the turf filler possible. He urged a delighted Mrs. Washburn to let her column run long today. Usually it was cut to the bone and she wrote him tart letters of complaint about the allegedly important items the editors had killed. He told Jim to start writing the Canfield story right away and he employed the services of a stenographer from the business office to type it out in takes as soon as Jim had finished a page of copy. It was going to be one of the most expensive editions the *Broadway Times* had ever issued, not only because of the lack of advertising revenue but because of the extra composing room cost of setting columns of unexpected copy. The skipper growled, but he put on three extra linotypers from the pool.

Inside an hour Slade called.

Like Blanton, Slade demanded an explanation. Hardin gave him the same explanation he had given Blanton.

Slade said, "I understand differently, Hardin. I understand it's the exact opposite, in fact. The plain inference I receive from certain persons of importance in the world of entertainment is that they resent the fact that you are supposedly closely associated with mobsters. It was a mistake for you to testify in behalf of that gangster yesterday, Hardin. It has created a very bad impression generally, I'm afraid. There are some ugly rumors abroad. Very ugly indeed."

Hardin shook his head. The bag of eels was really wriggling in an unexpected direction. Selig, in the terminology of pool sharks, was a master of reverse-English.

Hardin said, "I could hardly do anything else except testify. I saw the taxi driver at the time I said I did. Three other witnesses saw him, too."

"The other witnesses don't count," Slade retorted angrily. "All of them are connected with mobsters in one manner or another and their testimony would have carried no weight at all. It was your testimony that freed this gangster and book-

maker, Hardin. And personally I'm convinced that he was
guilty of murdering Jason Breck, who was a fine man and a
friend of mine. I really can't see that it was your moral or
civic duty to protect a gangster and I'm afraid you've made a
very grave mistake indeed. There's something else, Hardin,
something even worse, if possible. It's so bad that I don't think
I should discuss it on the phone. I think you had better come
over here to my apartment in Gracie Square."

Hardin said, "I'll come if you insist, of course. But if I
come there now, the *Broadway Times* won't get on the street
tonight. I'm already faced with sixteen wide-open columns to
fill with type and I understand there'll be more."

Slade said stiffly, "Well, if my employees can't come to me,
I suppose I can always come to them. My wife and I are supposed to attend a social gathering for cocktails in an hour or
so, but I'll come to see you at the office. Please wait for me."

"I'll wait," Hardin said and hung up the telephone.

Slade was obviously offended at his managing editor for
performing the duties he paid him to perform.

Hardin had barely hung up when the phone rang again.
This time it was the doctor Bart had engaged to attend the
Old Sarge. Eddie O'Grady, he learned, was resting comfortably. He was suffering from concussion but there was no skull
fracture. He would be hospitalized for several days, however.

Hardin worked steadily until Slade's arrival.

As soon as Slade strode into the office, he glanced meaning-
fully at old Jim Lennox. "This is strictly private, Hardin," he
declared. "I have come here at considerable personal incon-
venience to discuss this with you in private rather than by
phone, since you refused to come to my house."

Hardin banished old Jim to the city room and closed the
flimsy door of the beaverboarded cubicle that served him for
an office.

Slade was a very distinguished-looking man. His usually
bland and shrimp-pink face was dark with anger now and the
heavy black eyebrows beneath his silky white hair were knit
together. He sat down in a chair and said, "You're in very
bad trouble this time, Hardin. I have often warned you that
you are far too rash and impulsive, but I have always respected
you as a man of strict integrity, just the same. This time I'm
afraid you've gone off the deep end."

Slade took a long cigar from a leather case. The cigar was
enclosed in a glass holder. He shook it out of the glass holder

deliberately, clipped off the end, lit it with a gold lighter. When the cigar was drawing, he spoke again.

"Billy Beecher, the columnist, is running a very damaging item about you as the lead of his column tonight," Slade said. "I learned about the item from a close personal friend who is an executive of Beecher's paper. He tried to stop the thing because of his friendship for me, but he can't. Beecher's contract gives him the right to print anything he wants to print, apparently. This item states that you were bribed to testify for this bookmaker—what's his name, Merusi? It says that you met Merusi in a bar last evening, that witnesses observed you went into a private room with him and that you were paid a first installment of ten thousand dollars for your testimony. The item says further that you received a second payment of ten thousand dollars this afternoon."

Hardin made no answer. After a long silence, Slade said, "Well, Hardin?"

"Do you believe the story?" Hardin asked.

"I have told you that up to now, at any rate, I have always considered you a man of integrity," Slade replied. "However, it is not possible that Beecher would dare to print this unless there was some basis. He may be sued for libel at times and he may be irresponsible, but he is not that irresponsible, Hardin. He got this story from some sources that he can trust."

Hardin said, "I was in the Sligo Slasher's bar last night. Joe the Whistler came in. He said he wanted to speak to me privately and we went into a back room. He handed me an envelope with ten thousand dollars in it. I smashed him in the face and gave him back the money. You can verify at least part of that by looking at the Whistler's mouth. He refused to fight me. He said the money is his offer for a picture of a butterfly his younger brother had painted and given to me. He said he wanted to buy the butterfly."

Slade said, "This is nonsense, Hardin! Ten thousand for some amateur's painting of a butterfly!"

Hardin said, "I thought so, too, but he wanted it pretty badly. He said I could have ten grand more this afternoon if I would give him the picture of the butterfly. Last night some goons wanted the picture badly enough to slug an innocent old man and steal it."

"I never heard anything so completely incredible," Slade

fumed. "Why on earth would a gangster like that want a butterfly and why . . ."

He was interrupted by a light knock on the door. Hardin said, "Come in." The door opened and Bertha, the phone girl, batted her false eyelashes at him. She cast covert glances at Slade. Bertha said, "I couldn't find the copy boy, Mr. Hardin. One of the boys from a messenger service just delivered this. He said it was urgent, so I thought I'd better bring it back. I signed the receipt."

She handed Bart a thick Manila envelope. The envelope was tightly sealed and addressed to Hardin. There was no return address except the rubber stamp of the messenger service.

The flustered Bertha left hurriedly. Slade's eyes were narrowed and they were staring at Hardin. Bart ripped open the envelope. Inside was a thick package wrapped in brown paper. There was a sheaf of hundred-dollar bills inside. Hardin leafed through them as Slade expelled his breath in surprise. On top of the bills was a typed note.

The note read:

> Dear Hardin—Here's the extra ten grand I promised you. Thanks for everything. Your pal.
>
>   Joe Merusi.

Hardin handed the note to Slade.

Slade said, "Do you plan to return this money? I suppose it's rather like closing the barn door after the horse is stolen. The girl has signed for it and you have accepted it from her. Beecher's column will state that the second payment came to you this afternoon in a package from a messenger service. There will be a record of the delivery in the service's office, of course."

Hardin said, "I'll return it—in my own peculiar way."

Slade's voice was hard and cold now. "I'm afraid that's the trouble, Hardin," he said. "You insist on doing everything in your own peculiar way. You won't take advice. I've tried to help you, but it looks as if you've made your bed. Can you explain Merusi sending you this very large amount of money? You've told me you wouldn't even sell him this ridiculous butterfly."

"Merusi didn't send it," Hardin declared. "He may have been the one who gave it to the messenger service, but it wasn't Joe the Whistler's money. It was Selig's money. Selig has a grudge against me. I threw coffee in his face and he didn't like it much. He said he was going to run me off Broadway. Ten thousand isn't much to Selig when he really wants something."

"And you have prejudiced my interests and a valuable newspaper property as well as your own reputation and your job for the childish satisfaction of throwing coffee in a gangster's face?" asked Slade. "Just exactly what do you plan to do about all this, Hardin? I'd rather like to know."

Hardin said, "First, I plan to put a paper on the street if you'll give me time to do the work I'm paid for. After I do that, I plan to go out and prove that a man called Joe the Whistler committed two murders. He can't be tried again for one of them, but he can burn for the other if I can make it stick. If I prove Joe the Whistler is a murderer, it will accomplish several things. The only answer to pressure by the Syndicate is counter-pressure. If I can prove one of the Syndicate's big shots is a murderer, Selig will back down. Selig knows how to back down when he has to. He'll take the heat off me and the *Broadway Times*. That will solve your problem and it will prove I wasn't bribed."

"You would have to do this pretty quickly, Hardin. Before you're ruined and the paper is badly damaged. You would have to do it tonight, in fact."

"I intend to do it tonight," Hardin answered.

"And just how do you intend to accomplish this tonight, Hardin?" Slade asked.

"With a butterfly," Hardin answered.

If he could make good his boast, it would accomplish another important end, Bart thought. It would mean that Lieutenant Romano would not be forced to retire under a cloud.

There was just one thing wrong with his plan.

He had no idea at all just how he was going to prove the man he had saved from the electric chair was actually a murderer.

eleven

When Slade finally left, Hardin tossed the package of hundred-dollar bills carelessly into the drawer on top of the Irish-whisky bottle. Before he attacked the mountain of copy and proofs and cuts that lined his desk, he made a telephone call to Marty Land.

He said to Marty, "I want you to do two things for me. Call Hayden at the Saddle and Whip and reserve that table in the alcove again. Meet me there at seven-thirty tonight. This time I'll buy the dinner."

Marty agreed without asking questions.

Bart said, "Do you have any of your office stationery at home, Marty? The kind with your firm's name printed at the top?"

"I always keep some letterheads in the study," Marty answered. "Sometimes my secretary comes here for dictation when Marty has a hangover or other serious illness. Why?"

"Bring a sheet of stationery with you when you meet me tonight," Bart said, and hung up the phone.

For the next few hours Hardin worked steadily and he worked at top speed. He did not take his usual break at four to refresh himself at the Sligo Slasher's. He did push the ten thousand dollars aside, take out the Irish bottle and gulp from it, without even bothering to procure a paper cup. Late in the afternoon old Pops Taylor ambled into Bart's office, grinning.

"I've sent up all the time copy that's been accumulating in a bottom drawer since Dewey captured Manila," he declared. "From the looks of it, I think some of the stuff was here when I first arrived and that was forty years ago."

At six the last copy had hit the composing room and Bart climbed the stairs to make up the paper. Forms still stood around with gaping holes, awaiting the type from the ma-

110

chines. Bart ordered the proof room to railroad everything and get it in the forms regardless of typographical errors. At seven promptly the last form was locked and rolled to the stereotyper.

It would be the damnedest edition of the *Broadway Times* that had ever hit the street, Bart thought. There were stories about Richard Canfield and Lillian Russell and John Drew and Anna Held and Lou Tellegen. Turf had even sent up a long and scholarly article about Matchem, Herod and Eclipse, the three fountainhead sires that founded the long line of thoroughbreds. A newspaper was one of the few institutions that could rise to an emergency in this age of the forty-hour week, Hardin thought.

When the last form rolled, Hardin returned to his office to await the rattling of the windowpanes which would signal that the ancient presses were running. He found Jim Lennox waiting for him. "Why don't you go home, Jim?" he asked. "It's all wrapped up."

The old man looked at Bart solicitously. "You look tired, Bart," he said. "You worked hard today."

"I didn't get much sleep last night between one thing and another," Hardin said. "I doubt I'll get much tonight, either. But maybe after tomorrow I'll have a nice long vacation. You worked damned hard yourself, Jim, turning out all that copy. Yet you seem pretty chipper and you're twice my age."

The old man smiled happily. "I loved every minute of it," he replied. "It's wonderful to feel you're really useful. Sometimes I get to thinking that this job is just a kind of sinecure, that you're inventing things for me to do and don't really need my services."

Lennox wouldn't leave until the sample copies from the press came up. Hardin smiled. The old man was like a young cub reporter, eager to read in print the words he'd written.

Shortly before seven-thirty, Hardin left the office and went to the Saddle and Whip. Marty had reserved the alcove but he had not appeared. A press agent of one of the theatres that had canceled its advertising in the *Broadway Times* saw Bart, averted his eyes, and hurried away. Two overdressed Syndicate big shots looked at him, winked and began to whisper to each other. If Hayden had heard the unpleasant rumbles Selig had started on the Big Street, his broad, impassive face did not show it. He conducted Hardin to the alcove, summoned a waiter and told him to serve Mr. Hardin an Irish on the rocks immediately.

Hardin was sipping the drink when Marty arrived.

Marty sat down, ordered a very dry martini, and shook his head sadly at Hardin. "I always said that anybody who stays on the Street too long gets a little peculiar," he declared. "You're growing more mysterious by the hour, cousin, but I always find it best to humor little eccentricies." He reached in an inside pocket and produced a folded letterhead. "Here's the nice, blank piece of paper you wanted me to bring."

"Take a drink to steady your hand," Bart said, "then get out your pretty gold fountain pen and write down what I dictate."

Marty made a little ceremony of sipping the drink and producing the fountain pen. "I'm ready, chum," he said. "What do I do? Confess I kidnapped the long-lost Charley Ross?"

Bart thought a moment, then he said, "Write this. 'Received from Bart Hardin the sum of ten thousand dollars in final payment for legal services rendered to Joseph Merusi in connection with the case of The People Against Merusi."

Marty grinned happily. "You see?" he said. "Marty's never wrong. In the tropics it's the sun that gets them. On Broadway it's the glare of the electric signs."

He wrote what Bart had dictated.

Hardin reached into a sagging pocket and produced the packet of hundred-dollar bills. He shoved them toward Marty. "Date it and sign it," he said. "Wait a minute. I want a witness."

He called Hayden, the maître, to sign as witness. Hayden merely shrugged and signed. In his capacity as a headwaiter on Broadway he was used to curious requests.

Hardin ordered steak because he almost always ordered steak for dinner. Marty, who fancied himself a gourmet, ordered it because he said a man needed red meat when he was deprived of his proper rest.

Bart told Marty how the money had come to him and what had occurred that afternoon. Land said, "I don't know, Hardin. This thing has reached the point where I'm baffled completely. Busy Izzy, the perjured witness, was released this afternoon, as I predicted. Since the thing was just a pushover, I recommended that Selig engage the services of a young attorney who's just starting out. He's a graduate of Harvard Law, my own dear Alma Mater. I'm very Old School Tie, you know, despite the polka-dot bows I usually wear. Anyway, it didn't take the lad long. All he had to do was get affidavits from Buffo and Marsten to show that Izzy picked up the Whistler on the seventh instead of the eighth. He flashed those on Broderick, the D.A., and it was all over. Izzy is on the street again tonight."

"I think maybe I should see Busy Izzy," Bart said. "Do you know where I can find him?"

Marty shook his head. "I wouldn't know," he replied. "I would guess that the boys will keep him under wraps for a while. Of course, it's even possible that the boys may revert to their old customs and rub poor Izzy out, but since Selig was so concerned with the legal protection of Mr. Feldheim I would rather doubt that. Why do you want to see him, anyway?"

Bart said, "I'm just fishing. I'm going to try to prove that Joe the Whistler is a murderer, and I'm going to try to prove it tonight. Maybe it would help if I could prove he murdered Breck, even though he can't be tried again for that. It might mean that the police would see it Romano's way, that they would make reprisals by putting the heat on Joe the Whistler and Selig and the Syndicate and all the Syndicate's enterprises if they were convinced Joe had beaten the rap by making suckers out of them. They've done that before, not once but many times, and it's always worked, for a little while at least. The Syndicate has pulled in its ears and gone completely underground and has quit flexing its muscles out in public when the heat was on. If that happened, they'd take the heat off me and they'd take the heat off the *Broadway Times*, and Romano would be vindicated. But I really want to prove something that may be even harder. I want to prove that Joe the Whistler committed a crime for which he can be tried. I want to prove that the Whistler killed his brother."

"If you do," said Marty, "I'm rather afraid that this time I won't be around to defend him. I've about come to the conclusion that you and Romano and the D.A.'s office weren't the only suckers in the Breck case. I think the Syndicate made a big, fat sucker out of Marty, too, even if it did pay him a fat retainer of forty thousand for taking the case and has just paid off its promised bonus of another ten, somewhat reluctantly, perhaps, through your good offices. Marty is vain. He doesn't like being made a sucker. Marty has just about decided he needs a rest and is going to take a Caribbean cruise. A nice, long Caribbean cruise."

"The butterfly has got to be the missing link in this," Bart said. "I don't know how or why, but it's the piece that's

missing. If we only knew why Joe and the Syndicate wanted
the butterfly that Benny gave me at this table just last night,
I think we'd have something that would stick."

Marty smiled. "I never thought a butterfly as a missing
link before," he said. "The popular conception of a missing
link is slightly more anthropoid, a cross between an ape and
a human being. Moe Selig fills the bill almost perfectly."

Hardin called for the check after they had finished a dessert
of strawberries soaked in kirsch which Marty, in his role of
gourmet, recommended as a rare delicacy. Marty insisted on
paying the check. He said he wanted to get one of his pretty
new hundred-dollar bills changed.

Land left Hardin outside the restaurant at a quarter to nine,
which is barely twilight in the world called Broadway. He
swore he was going home, bolt the door, disconnect the telephone, and sleep for twelve straight hours.

Hardin stood uncertainly for several minutes outside the
restaurant. Several passersby, men he knew in the world of
the theatre, spoke to him hurriedly and glanced at him covertly. I'm getting the Treatment, he thought. Usually you
don't last long on Broadway when you get the Treatment.
When there's a rumble that you're on your way out, people
flee you as if you wore leper bells around your neck.

Few men survive the Treatment on the Big Street, whose
frenetic tempo is pitched to the pursuit of the fast buck,
where quick, sensational success alone ranks as accomplish-
ment. Hardin saw a man he knew, a man who was thin,
intense and flashily dressed. He looked at Hardin briefly,
barely nodded, hurried by. He was a quondam booking agent
who had come on evil days through drink and gambling.
Almost always when he saw Bart he approached him with
a kind of frantic cordiality, spoke of vague money-making
schemes that he was about to put into execution, and wound
up by borrowing a few dollars. When the panhandlers quit
bracing you on Broadway, you're finished, Bart thought.

A wind with the chill of winter in it gusted up the lighted
canyon. Hardin shivered. He'd have to remember to attach
the woolen lining in his trenchcoat, he thought. A newsboy
came by with the bulldog editions of the morning papers.
Hardin bought the tab in which Billy Beecher's column
appeared, leafed through it under the lights of the restaurant's sign. The story was there, all right, although Beecher
had shown unaccustomed caution in not using Hardin's name.

As he held the paper, Bart cursed himself because his hand

was trembling slightly. Even though he was an editor of a
Broadway paper he never had quite realized before that every
day people on this street opened newspapers, not with the
casual interest of the breakfast-table reader, but with fear and
trembling, as if they were about to read their fate in a Book
of Doom. Reviews of plays could mean the making or losing
of fortunes for producers and the critical opinions expressed
in print could start young actors and actresses soaring to the
stars or send them back to some small town, hopeless and
defeated. There must also be a daily, dreadful rite of famous
people searching the gossip columns and praying that their
private sins had not suddenly become public. Bart read the
item that was the lead-all of Beecher's column.

> *One of the witnesses who appeared for the defense in
> the murder trial of a well-known bookmaker is a news-
> boy who likes to dabble with cards and dice and bet the
> horses. Frequently borrows from the mob's loan sharks
> at 6 for 5. Rumbles are he can bet without borrowing for
> quite a spell. Had appointment with the defendant in a
> bar across from Madison Square Garden the other eve-
> ning and quite a bundle changed hands when they went
> into a back room. Another bundle arrived from the bookie
> by special messenger in the afternoon. The defense wit-
> ness likes fancy vests. He can buy some real pretty ones
> with 20 Gees.*

It was typical Beecher, Bart thought. Just enough truth
was in it to make the entire story appear credible. Bart liked
to gamble, he had occasionally borrowed money from Selig,
who was a loan shark as well as a bookmaker, at 6 for 5 interest, he had been in the back room of a bar with Joe the
Whistler, and he had received a "bundle" from a messenger
service that afternoon.

Hardin stuffed the paper in his pocket and went into a
cigar store. He entered a phone booth and dialed the number
of Manhattan West. Romano was on duty. His voice was
flat and despondent. Hardin told Romano he was coming
down to see him.

He left the cigar store and flagged a cab.

Bart found Romano in his office, sitting in a squeaky swivel
chair behind a scarred old desk. He looked tired and his dark
eyes were lifeless. Hardin gestured toward a cracked and
ancient leather couch that had been among the furnishings

of Romano's office as long as he could remember. "You look as if you'd been sleeping on the couch again," he said. Romano nearly always slept on the couch when he was in charge of a murder case that was breaking.

Romano nodded. "Yeah," he said. "A man gets habits. I been sitting here waiting for a break, like always, but it's kind of silly. They took me off the Merusi case last night. They put a young detective on it. He's one of the new kind. He's got a college education and he dresses so good you couldn't tell him from a customer's man in Wall Street."

Romano had been holding a small bottle in his hand when Bart entered. He shook a pill from it into his hand, poured water from a thermos jug, and took the pill. He said, "What do you want? If it's about the Whistler's brother, I don't know. They got a system down here now. Nobody tells Romano anything. They think Romano ain't quite bright."

Hardin said, "I came to join the cops."

"There ought to be a vacancy some time tomorrow afternoon," the lieutenant replied. "Usually the Commissioner plays golf on Saturday afternoon. He's a real good golfer, I understand. Shoots somewhere in the low eighties, they tell me. The Commissioner hates to miss an afternoon of golf, but tomorrow he's seeing me instead. He sent old Inspector Sansone down to tell me. When old Sansone carries a message from the Commissioner in person, it's real important. Old Sansone is supposed to be the toughest cop in town and he's the Commissioner's white-haired boy."

"I understand they let Busy Izzy out this afternoon," Bart said.   . . . .

Romano nodded heavily. "Yeah," he said. "They let Joe the Whistler out because Busy Izzy told a lie. Then they let Busy Izzy out because they found he didn't tell a lie, or didn't mean to, anyway. Sometimes the law can be a funny thing."

"I want to find Izzy," Bart said. "You know where he might be?"

Romano shook his head. "He might be driving his little taxicab and he might be dead," he said. "I wouldn't know. Like I say, they don't tell Romano anything because Romano don't like the Syndicate and wants to get real tough and they're afraid he might. All I know is that when this Izzy came to us with his perjured testimony he was living in a flea bag on Jacobs Beach called the Buckingham Chambers."

Bart said, "I know that place. Old Pops Taylor insists on

living there. I don't know why, except it's convenient to the office and all the better crap games."

Romano didn't seem very interested. He said, "You ever try to fry an ice cube in a red-hot skillet, Hardin?"

"What?" Bart asked.

"That's what I been doing lately. Frying ice cubes in a red-hot skillet," Romano declared. "It's not much fun. It's what you call frustrating. One minute you've got something nice and solid in your hand, and then you put the heat on it and it just disappears. The same thing happens when you're chump enough to try to put the heat on a guy like Joe the Whistler or to buck the Syndicate all by yourself. First you've got it, but the minute the heat goes on, it's gone. If they'd have given me Joe the Whistler for just a little while last night, I might have broken two murder cases. I had him, I had him right in my hand. But when I come down here and started to make with the heat, I find this young assistant D.A., Saltus, waiting for me, and all of a sudden Joe the Whistler disappears, just like the ice cube, and next I've got an appointment with the Commissioner because I ever brought Joe down in the first place. I don't think the Commissioner is missing his golf game just to give me a promotion, Hardin. Honest, I don't."

Bart thought a minute. Finally he said, "I've got a lot to tell you, Romano. You say nobody is telling you anything, but I'm going to tell you everything I know and I hope to God it may help you to remember something about the butterfly, the thing you say that you forgot. You haven't remembered about the butterfly since last night, have you?"

Romano shook his head. "No," he said. "I guess I must have had a dream about a butterfly, or maybe there was a butterfly in some other case a long time ago. Sansone, who's a hell of a lot older than I am and hasn't retired yet, tells me the Commissioner thinks I'm getting a little old."

Hardin told Romano everything that had happened since he had seen him at the art museum the night before.

When he had finished, all Romano said was, "I don't know what it means except that you're right up behind the eight-ball, the same way I am."

"When you're behind the eight-ball you make a bank shot," Hardin retorted. "Maybe we can bank off Busy Izzy."

"Bank shots are okay in a game of straight pool," Romano said, "but when you're up against sharks, you play dirty pool.

That's what I was going to do, play dirty pool. Only they wouldn't let me."

"You can't just quit," Bart urged. "Come on. We'll play dirty pool. Get up off your tail and we'll go find Izzy."

For just a moment Romano's dark eyes lighted up. Then they became dead again and he shook his head. "No," he said. "There isn't any use. It's too late now, anyway. It won't do any good for me to stick my neck out any farther. I stretched it too far already."

"Nuts," said Hardin. "There's still a chance. If we can make Izzy talk and find out why he sat on that witness stand and perjured himself to hell and back and risked getting killed by the mob, we may have something. Maybe it will help us figure out the reason Joe the Whistler wanted the butterfly. Maybe it will help us prove that Joe the Whistler murdered Jason Breck and killed his brother Benny. Anyway, we can try. The time is getting short, Romano. You can't just sit there."

Romano's chair creaked slightly as he leaned back. "I'm going to sit here," he declared. "I'm going to sit here in this squeaky chair like I've always done when they threw a murder in my lap. I'm going to wait for the breaks. This time there won't be any breaks, but I'll sit here just the same, because a man gets habits. Maybe it's the last time that I'll sit here. Maybe next week they'll have a new cop in the chair, one of those young detectives with a college education." The lieutenant's eyes scanned the little room, the cracked walls with their mustard-colored paint, the sagging leather couch, the lamp with the green glass shade. "It's not a very pretty place," he said. "But I'm kind of used to it."

"All right," Hardin said desperately. "If you won't come, I'll go out alone. I'm going to find Busy Izzy and I'm going to make him talk. Maybe it will work and maybe it won't, but I'm going to try. You must be able to help me at least a little bit. You must know something that I ought to know, even if you can't remember about the butterfly. You were in charge of the Breck murder squeal and you put the collar on Joe the Whistler."

Romano sighed. "I didn't have enough to go to court," he answered. "I had almost enough, but Izzy Feldheim came along and made his statement and that was all the D.A. wanted. I told him that maybe it wasn't quite enough because Busy Izzy was a rat and rats don't make good witnesses. But the D.A. wouldn't listen. He thought he had it on ice, especially since Joe the Whistler wouldn't even offer us an alibi. Not even a phony alibi. The D.A. was so sure, he didn't even bother to try the case himself like he usually would do with a big-time mobster he's been gunning for for years. He sent one of his office boys, this Saltus, to court instead."

Romano closed his heavy-lidded eyes and tilted back in the swivel chair. He said, "There's not much I can tell you except one thing. I got a big Italian nose in the middle of my face. It smells real good. When they found Breck's body and the squeal came in, I smelled Joe the Whistler. When they found Benny beneath that statue with his head split open last night, I smelled Joe the Whistler again. Joe the Whistler is a killer. He's killed twice already and maybe he'll kill again before he's through. But the D.A. and the Commissioner are covering up. They put a lying witness on the stand and they want everybody to forget that as quick as possible. They won't let me make a grab at Joe the Whistler. So I'll just sit here. Maybe there'll be a break, even now, even though it don't seem possible. Sometimes it happens like a miracle. Anyhow, I'll sit and wait because it's the only thing there is to do."

Bart rose. "All right," he said, "I'm leaving. Since you're going to be here, I may call in in case there's anything to tell you."

"There's no reason for me to leave," Romano said. "I've got everything I need right here. I've got a lumpy couch to lie down on if I get tired and I've got a hot plate and a jar instant coffee and I've got a bottle of pills to quiet my nervous stomach."

Bart said, "So long, Romano."

The lieutenant grinned feebly. "So long, Hardin. Give my regards to Busy Izzy if you find him."

Hardin had to walk to Eighth Avenue to find a cab. He told the driver to drop him off at Forty-ninth.

The Buckingham Chambers was a bleak and forbidding building. It stood next to the Catholic church that loomed so incongruously in the middle of the thoroughfare called Jacobs Beach. Bart walked into the lobby of the shabby hotel. A man with a pockmarked face and broken teeth lounged behind the desk reading a tabloid. Since Pops Taylor lived in the hotel, Hardin knew the night clerk. His name was Grulik. When Bart went to the desk, Grulik looked up and a smile spread over his face.

"I see you're real famous, pal," Grulik said. "I see you made Billy Beecher's column in the blats. You got to be a real big shot for Billy Beecher to write you up. If you're looking for Pops Taylor, he ain't in. He was itching for some action and he heard the boys was playing blackjack uptown somewhere. Friday's Pops' payday and Pops always gets restless on his payday."

"I wasn't looking for Pops," Bart said. "I was looking for another tenant of yours. Izzy Feldheim."

"Oh," said Grulik. His eyes were suddenly veiled. "That character checked out of here weeks ago, when he got to be a famous stool pigeon."

"You know where I might find him?"

Grulik said, "When you get to be a clerk in a pad like this, you never know nothing when people ask questions, pal. That way you keep on working. That way you keep on living, too. I guess maybe a lot of parties are looking for Busy Izzy tonight."

"You wouldn't have an idea where they might be looking, would you?" Bart asked, laying a ten-dollar bill conspicuously on the desk in front of Grulik.

Grulik said, "I don't know much. I know sometimes he used to go across the river to Jersey to see the burlesque shows. Sometimes he played the sidestreet traps, the ones where bargain broads hang around and wait for customers. I know he used to play a trap called the Wooden Shoe on Forty-fifth. I don't know a sawbuck's worth, pal."

Bart said, "Keep it anyway. Maybe I'll be back. Maybe you'll remember something."

Grulik said, "Thanks, pal. If you find the character, tell him we saved a room for him."

Bart started for the door.

Grulik called after him, "Hey, pal! You know something?"

Bart turned, said, "What?"

Grulik said, "I wouldn't be surprised if that Busy Izzy was dead as vaudeville by now. Why don't you try the undertaking parlors?"

twelve

It was ten-thirty when Hardin crossed Eighth Avenue to the west side of the street. He glanced at the lighted marquee of Madison Square Garden. Two middleweight contenders were fighting tonight. They were fair boys, but Hardin suspected the arena was half empty. Boxers on the Friday shows were strictly television actors nowadays. The enormous lobby of the Garden and the sidewalk outside were deserted. Bart had hoped he might see Tom Trigg hanging around in front of the place as usual. Tom was an old Negro who had fought the best heavies of his time. He haunted the entrance to the scene of his triumphs like a spectre, as a rule. He heard most of the rumbles on the street and Bart thought he might have a lead to Busy Izzy's present whereabouts. He wasn't around tonight. Maybe they'd let him inside for free because of the many empty seats. Maybe he was warming himself with gin in some nearby bar.

Hardin headed down Eighth Avenue. The Wooden Shoe was a dark and grimy little place west of Eighth. The only excuse for its name appeared to be a wooden shoe advertising a Holland beer which the proprietor used as a window decoration.

Hardin had to descend two steps below street level to enter. The bar was in a sub-basement. Inside, the place was smoky twilight. The bar seemed to have a mixed clientele. An effeminate chorus boy with marcelled hair looked up eagerly as Bart entered. So did a dead-eyed woman with a painted face and breasts that were impossibly protuberant beneath her sweater. A small Puerto Rican in a bright-blue suit sat alone at a little table, staring fixedly at the woman in the sweater and drinking beer. The jacket of the bright-blue suit was so wide in the shoulder it might have been tailored for Rocky Marciano. Two youthful sailors were attempting awkwardly

121

to make conversation with the woman. She had evidently decided that while their intentions were dishonorable enough, their bankrolls were strictly limited. She was playing the chill for them.

The bartender was thin and dark and sharp-faced. He wore a bullfighter's sideburns that reached to his jowls. The bartender regarded Bart suspiciously.

As Hardin walked to the bar, one of the young sailors took hold of the woman's arm and said, "What's the matter, lady? Why don't you want to have a beer with us?"

The woman shook off the boy's hand without anger. "Why don't you two big spenders drop a dime in the juke box or something? I drink Scotch," she said.

She carried her highball glass up the bar, put it down beside Hardin. "Hello, man," she said. "It seems my glass is empty."

Hardin looked sidelong at her, said to the bartender, "Fill the lady's glass. I'll take Irish. The kind that's not watered, if you've got it. Put it on the rocks."

When the bartender served the drinks, Bart shoved a bill toward him. "I'm looking for someone who comes in here," he said.

"Lots of people come in here, mister," the bartender replied.

"The one I'm looking for is named Izzy Feldheim. They call him Busy Izzy. He's a cab driver."

"He's not here," the bartender said. He said it rapidly, as if the answer were an automatic reaction to the stimulus of a question.

"Has he been in tonight?" Bart persisted.

The bartender was wiping the bar with a towel. "Don't know him," he said.

"If you don't know him, how do you know he's not here?" Bart asked.

"Because I know the people who are here, mister."

"You don't know me," Bart said.

The woman had already gulped most of her drink. She said, "Why don't you tell the nice man the truth, Eddie? Why don't you tell him Izzy's dead by now?"

The bartender glared at her. He said to Bart, "She's on the weed. When they're on the weed, they talk, but the words they talk don't mean a thing."

The woman said pleasantly, "You know what you are,

Eddie? You're a louse. You're a filthy, dirty louse with whiskers."

She turned to Bart. "I'll tell you something, dear," she said. "Izzy was in here a couple of hours ago. He was coming home with me. Then two of Selig's torpedoes came in and he went out with them. You think Izzy's still alive if he went out with a couple of Selig's torpedoes a couple of hours ago?"

"Dames on the weed," the bartender said disgustedly. "They like suicide the hard way."

"Izzy wasn't a bad guy," the woman declared. "He was a friend of mine. He came up to see me." She put her glass down. "My glass is empty again, mister," she said.

"Give the lady another drink," Hardin said to the bartender.

The bartender shrugged. "Sure," he said. "Maybe it's better if you die drunk."

"Just in case Izzy is still alive, do you know any place he might be?" Bart asked the woman.

"He said he was going to check into the Buckingham Chambers again," the woman replied. "He used to live there before the cops started paying his rent. He liked the bars with B-girls. You might try Fatty's Place on Forty-fourth. But you won't find him, mister. He and I were going to have a little party to celebrate him being out again, but those two came in and they talked to him a minute and he went out with them."

Bart shoved a five-dollar bill in front of the woman. "Have a few on me," he said. "I'll take a look in Fatty's Place."

The bartender's hard eyes followed Bart as he left.

Fatty's Place was just off Eighth Avenue. It was much larger and much more brightly lighted than the Wooden Shoe. It fairly glittered. In the trade it was called a flash trap. Electric lights gleamed nakedly on mirrors and white tile and chromium fixtures. The room was long and narrow and booths with tables and red plastic seats lined the entire wall space that wasn't occupied by the long bar. Nearly all of the booths had occupants. The occupants were mostly soldiers and sailors and girls whose frilly dinner gowns and lack of coats and hats indicated they were employed by the management, despite local ordinances and ABC regulations against such practice. The waitresses were made up like showgirls and wore tight-fitting uniforms with very short skirts. There was a juke box

at each end of the long, narrow room and both were blaring
raucous rock-'n'-roll music.

A man in sporty clothes who was obviously the proprietor
strode up and down the big room. He wore a large carnation
in his buttonhole and he was built along the general lines of
an outsize hogshead. As Hardin entered, the man approached
him and said, "Welcome to Fatty's Place, mister. Bar or
table?"

Hardin loosened the belt of his trenchcoat and Fatty
looked curiously at his fancy vest. "Hey!" he exclaimed.
"Aren't you Hardin of the *Broadway Times?* I thought you
looked familiar. Couldn't miss that vest. Step right up to the
bar and have the best in the house on Fatty."

Hardin said, "I was looking for somebody I thought might
be here. A cab driver called Busy Izzy."

Fatty's conscientiously jovial face hardened. "Take my
advice, chum," he said. "Don't look."

"Why?" asked Hardin.

"Because you're young and healthy. Stay healthy, boy.
Like Fatty always says, you got only one body. Take care of it.
You take me now. I'm not really fat. I'm like old Tony
Galento." Fatty slapped his beer belly. "All bone and muscle.
Work out in the gym twice a week. Never smoke or drink
the stuff I sell the suckers. Stay healthy, that's what Fatty
says. You step up to the bar and have fun. Or sit down in a
booth and I'll bring a nice young lady to talk to you. How
about it?"

"I don't want a nice young lady," Bart replied. "I want
Izzy."

"No, mister. Now I think of it, I never heard of him.
You take Fatty's advice. Stay healthy, chum."

Bart said, "Thanks. I'll go right out and buy myself a
batch of vitamins."

He turned his back on Fatty and left the bar.

He walked east on Forty-fourth to Broadway. This block
was almost solid with theatres and the streets were thronged
by men and women who had spilled out for the second inter-
mission. They smoked and elbowed each other and chattered.
Hardin made slow progress pushing his way through the
theatre crowds. He turned left on Broadway and walked to
the main entrance of the Astor. He spoke to the doorman,
who wore a braided ankle-length coat and visored cap.

"Hello, Murphy," Hardin said. "How are the wife and
kids?"

"Fine, fine, Mr. Hardin. The oldest boy graduates from high school next spring. I think he's going to be an atomic scientist or something. He's real good in chemistry."

"Murphy, does a driver called Busy Izzy ever hack this stand?" Bart asked.

"Sure," said Murphy. "He used to hack it pretty regular. But I haven't seen him since he started living on the cops."

"Not working tonight, then?"

Murphy said, "I haven't seen him. He hacks for Red Feather Cabs. They've got their garage on Ninth and Fiftieth. You might ask there. Excuse me, Mr. Hardin."

Murphy opened the door of a cab that had just pulled up. When he returned, he said, "There's a kind of rumble about Izzy around, Mr. Hardin."

"What rumble?"

Murphy hesitated. "I don't usually pay much attention to rumbles," he said. "I don't repeat them. You keep your mouth shut on this street, you last a lot longer. But the rumble I heard was that certain parties were looking for Izzy a little while ago. That's all I know. There may be nothing to it."

"Thanks," said Bart. "I'll ask at the garage. Don't let that kid of yours blow you up with an atom bomb, Murphy."

He walked uptown, turned down Jacobs Beach again. He went into the Buckingham Chambers. Grulik was still behind the desk. Bart said, "I heard Izzy was planning to check in here again, Grulik. Has he arrived?"

Grulik looked at Bart for a moment, then he leaned over the desk and made sure the lobby was vacant.

"Pops Taylor got paid today," he said. "You work for the same blat, so you must have got paid, too. Everybody got paid but Grulik today, it seems."

Bart waited. Grulik waited, too. Then he picked up the tabloid and began to read it.

Hardin said, "How much, Grulik?"

Grulik put down the paper. He looked around apprehensively again. "It's funny," he said. "It's funny. About half a yard always helps Grulik to remember."

"You've had ten," Bart said. "Forty more is half a yard."

Grulik nodded, licked his lips and waited.

Hardin put down two twenties. Grulik picked them up.

Grulik said, "Certain parties were looking for Izzy a little while ago. One of the certain parties is a gun named Charley. Sometimes he does little jobs for Selig and Joe the Whistler and the organization. Not too often nowadays, but sometimes. The guy with him is a character called Boston. He's a gun, too, I understand. I hear they found what they were looking for. In that Wooden Shoe trap I told you about. The joint on Forty-fifth."

"That's not worth much," Hardin said. "I already knew that much. Where have they got Izzy now?"

Grulik said, "Listen, Hardin. I ain't a crystal gazer. I sold you all I've got to sell. They were looking and they found what they were looking for, that's all I know. Maybe they fixed up Izzy with a broad to keep him occupied. Maybe they're playing cards with him. Maybe they sent him off for a nice vacation. Maybe Izzy's kind of dead, who knows? But I don't think so. The way I get it, they don't want Izzy dead just yet. They just want him nice and quiet."

Hardin nodded. Maybe Grulik knew more. Maybe he didn't. It was obvious that anything else he knew was not for sale, at any rate.

Bart walked out to the street. He headed up Eighth Avenue to Fiftieth. The fight crowd was streaming out of the Garden now. As usual, there were murmurs of fixes and dives. Hardin wondered idly who had won, but he didn't care enough to ask. On Fiftieth he walked west.

He found the Red Feather Taxi garage on Ninth Avenue. A dim light was burning in the office. Hardin went inside. The company was reputedly a Syndicate enterprise. Hardin knew he might be walking into trouble.

The dispatcher was a beefy man who wore black-rimmed glasses. He glared at Hardin suspiciously and said, "You want something?"

"I'm trying to find one of your drivers. Isadore Feldheim. They call him Busy Izzy."

The dispatcher's face became more wary. He was silent for a minute, thinking about it. Finally he said, "Who wants him?"

"My name is Hardin. Bart Hardin of the *Broadway Times*."

There was another silence while the dispatcher thought that over. He nodded. He said, "Wait a minute. I'll check in back."

The dispatcher walked through an open door. He closed the door behind him. He picked up a telephone and dialed. When he got an answer, he said, "This is Red Feather. A guy named Hardin's here. He's asking for Busy Izzy." He listened, then he said, "Okay, will do."

The dispatcher signaled to two men in the back of the garage who might have been mechanics. He opened the door again and crossed to the railing where Hardin was waiting. He said, "I checked. Feldheim's working tonight. He's due to come in any minute. Come on back here and sit down. You won't have long to wait."

He pushed open a gate in the fenced-off enclosure.

Hardin hesitated. Two men had come up from the dark recesses of the garage. They did not approach him. They stood casually between Hardin and the street door.

Hardin went into the dispatcher's enclosure and sat down.

The dispatcher said, "I got a bottle in the drawer. You want a drink?"

Hardin said, "No, thanks."

"It's getting cold outside," the dispatcher remarked.

Hardin said it was.

After that there was a long silence.

There was a big clock ticking on the wall. It was almost eleven-thirty. From somewhere, a long way off, there was the sound of music on a radio. One of the men who stood between Hardin and the street door was humming very softly. The other man was silent. His shadow loomed large upon the wall.

The dispatcher picked up a newspaper and began to read the comic page. The paper rustled in his hand. Once he looked up at Hardin. "It won't be long," he said reassuringly.

The clock on the wall ticked loudly. It ticked for seventeen minutes before a big car came roaring into the garage.

The car was not a taxicab. It was a private car, a two-tone Chrysler Imperial, Bart noted.

Three men got out of the car.

The first man was Joe the Whistler.

Hardin wondered if the other two were the guns called Charley and Boston.

The man in the horn-rimmed glasses put down his newspaper. He rose and stood waiting as the Whistler advanced toward the dispatcher's counter.

The Whistler nodded to the dispatcher, said, "Hello, Harvey."

He pushed open the gate and walked over to Hardin. The other two men remained outside the railing.

The Whistler said, "Hello, Hardin. What are you doing here? I hear you came into a bundle of the coarse today. You gonna buy the taxi company, maybe?"

Hardin did not rise. He said, "Hello, Whistler."

The Whistler said, "You know something, Hardin? I kind of like you. You gave me fat lip, but I like you just the same. You play it rough. That's the way I always play it, too."

"That's nice," said Hardin.

"I hear you've been asking questions, Hardin. I don't think you've been getting answers. I'm going to give you answers. Just because I like you."

"Thanks a million," Hardin said.

"What do you want with Busy Izzy, Hardin?" the Whistler asked. "You want to give him a fat lip, too?"

"I just want to have a friendly chat with him," Hardin replied.

"No reason you shouldn't, Hardin. No reason at all."

"Except I can't find him," Bart said.

"He's in room 715 of the Mid-City Hotel," the Whistler said. "He'll be there for a while. Knock before you go in, though. There's a lady with him."

The Whistler grinned. "I had the boys keep tabs on him," he said. "I didn't want anything to happen to him. If anything happened to him that cop Romano might blame me. Sometimes I think Romano don't like me very much."

"Room 715, Mid-City Hotel," Bart said.

The Whistler nodded. "That's right. The boys and I are driving downtown. We could drop you off if you wanted."

Bart said, "Thanks, I enjoy walking."

"Don't walk down any dark streets, Hardin," the Whistler urged. "They tell me there's a lot of lawlessness around."

"I'll be careful," Hardin said.

"You did me a favor yesterday," the Whistler declared. "Now I've done you one. I'm glad to see you're getting smart, Hardin. I thought you might try to give back that bundle you got this afternoon."

The Whistler opened the little gate and started to walk away.

Hardin rose from the chair. "Just a minute, Whistler," he called. "I want to show you something."

The Whistler turned toward Hardin. Bart took the receipt Marty Land had signed from his pocket. He handed it to the Whistler. He said, "I did a little errand for you today. I paid a bill you owed."

The Whistler examined the paper silently. Then he handed it back to Hardin. "You won't get mad if I tell you something, will you?" the Whistler asked.

"I won't get mad," Hardin promised.
The Whistler grinned amiably at Bart.
"Hardin," he said, "you're a real mean S.O.B."
Joe the Whistler walked toward the car.
He was whistling through his teeth.

thirteen

The Chrysler Imperial with the three men in it backed out into the street, turned on screeching tires, headed west.

Hardin said to the man in the horn-rimmed glasses, "Thanks."

The dispatcher was reading his paper again. He nodded and said, "It was nothing. Always glad to oblige a friend of the Whistler's."

Bart walked through the gate and headed toward the door of the garage. The two men who might be garage mechanics were still standing near the door. The dispatcher inclined his head almost imperceptibly. The two men allowed Hardin to walk out into the street.

Bart glanced at his watch and saw it lacked a minute or two of midnight. He wanted a telephone and a telephone wasn't too easy to find in this neighborhood at this time of night. He stood for a moment, peering down the street.

The man named Charley had jumped out of the car while it was still in motion. He was watching Hardin from a doorway. He saw Hardin go into a dingy bar. He could watch the entrance to the bar very comfortably from his post, so he did not move.

Hardin found the phone booth and dialed the number of Manhattan West. When he got Romano on the line, he said, "In ten or fifteen minutes I'll be in room 715 of the Mid-City Hotel. I've heard I'll find Busy Izzy there. Joe the Whistler volunteered the information. so I don't know just what I may be walking into. If I don't call you inside an hour, maybe you'd better check up."

Romano said, "Maybe I better come with you after all. They don't tell me anything but they still let me carry a gun."

"No," said Bart. "Having you along might be protection for me, if I need protection, but it would spoil the show. Our only hope is for me to get Izzy alone for a little while and make him talk. There's one chance in a thousand I can do it, and I've got to take the chance. The Mid-City is a Syndicate hotel. If you walked in, I think Izzy would disappear before we could reach the seventh floor, if he's really there to begin with."

"You want me to wait a whole hour?" Romano asked. "Lots of nasty things can happen in an hour."

"I think it's going to take that long," Bart answered. "Take a pill for your nervous stomach and wait there for my call."

He went out of the bar and stood on the curbing, looking for a cruising cab.

When the man in the doorway realized that Hardin was about to flag a cab, he grinned. That angle was taken care of, too. A cab from the company's garage had moved up to the curbing, just a little down the street. Hugging the building and its shadow, Charley went down the street and got into the cab. He saw Hardin enter a yellow taxi and he told the Red Feather driver to follow.

Hardin dismissed the cab at Forty-first and Ninth and walked west. Charley followed at a distance.

The Mid-City Hotel looked like any other second-rate hostelry in a big city except that it was more weatherbeaten.

Hardin stood on the sidewalk a moment, peering curiously into the lobby, remembering the card game that had been held here in September, the night that Jason Breck was murdered.

So it's going to end where it began, he thought.

He made a small prayer to Tyche, the Goddess of Gamblers, and entered the hotel.

There was not a soul in the lobby except the night clerk behind the desk.

Hardin did not see Sleeth, the day manager who had testified at the trial. Sleeth was in a small office behind the night clerk. The door to the small office was open a crack. Sleeth sat at a desk, looking strained and uncomfortable. The man called Boston sat in a straight chair beside the desk, looking bored, and yawning. Joe the Whistler was standing at the door, peering cautiously through the crack.

The Whistler watched Hardin for a moment, then he

closed the door softly and said, "Hardin's here. He went straight to the elevator."

"What do we do now?" asked Boston, stifling a yawn.

"We wait," said Joe the Whistler. "We wait till he comes down."

He nodded curtly to Sleeth. "Tell the desk man to ring you when he comes down," he said. "You got a drink in this lousy pad, Sleeth?"

A Negro elevator operator with a mask-like, frozen face took Hardin to the seventh floor. Bart found room 715 and tapped lightly on the door. He heard furtive movements in the room. A woman spoke softly. Hardin knocked again.

Someone came to the door but did not open it. A man's voice, close to the door panel, called, "What is it?"

"Open up," said Hardin. "Joe the Whistler sent me."

There was a short silence, then the man's voice said, "Just a minute, just a minute."

Hardin didn't wait a minute. He pounded the door hard.

It was opened by Busy Izzy. Busy Izzy wore trousers and an undershirt. He tried to block Hardin. He cried, "Hey, what the hell is this?"

Hardin shoved Izzy hard and walked into the room.

A blonde girl was pulling a dress down over her head. She looked at Bart and said angrily, "Listen, I pay off the house man in this pad! What you mean barging in like this?"

Bart nodded toward the door. "Out," he said to the girl.

The girl stood for a moment and stared defiantly at Bart. Then she dropped her eyes and hurriedly picked up a scarlet coat and a blue beret from a chair.

Izzy cried, "Don't you leave, baby! This guy's a nobody. A Goddamn newspaperman. You stay with me."

The girl shook her head and started for the door. "This guy is trouble, mister," she declared. "I don't want trouble."

Busy Izzy darted to the telephone, picked it up. Bart grabbed the cord of the phone, twisted it around his hand, jerked it out of the wall.

"Sit down, Izzy," he said. "You and I've got things to talk about."

"I got nothing to talk about with you! You get out of here!" Izzy said loudly.

Hardin drew his right arm deliberately back over his left shoulder. He smacked Izzy in the face with the back of his hand. Izzy spun around and collapsed on the rumpled bed.

Hardin drew his left arm back and smacked the other side of Izzy's face.

Izzy screamed, "Don't! Don't! I'm an old man!"

"You're not much more than forty, Izzy. But I'm a little younger and I'm a lot bigger," Bart said calmly. "I was a Marine and you learn some real dirty ways of fighting in the Marines."

He sliced the side of his hand down like a cleaver blade on Izzy's shoulder near the neck. Izzy squealed, grabbed the shoulder and rolled back on the bed, huddled like a foetus and groaning softly.

Hardin said, "The next time I do that, the collarbone breaks, Izzy. A broken collarbone can hurt like hell."

"Why are you belting me?" Izzy sobbed. "I never did nothing to you. What you want of me?"

"I want you to talk, Izzy. You'd better start talking pretty quick. I want you to tell me why you went on that witness stand. You're going to talk. I'm going to make you. Joe the Whistler won't protect you. Joe the Whistler told me where to find you."

"I don't believe it!" Izzy cried hysterically. "You know I can't tell you. You know what they'd do to me!"

"They're not here, Izzy," Bart said calmly. "I'm here. I know what I'm going to do to you."

Izzy cowered against the wall, his arms drawn up protectively, his hands pressed against his face. The eyes that stared at Hardin were wild and fear-crazed.

Hardin leaned casually over the bed. He sank his fist in Izzy's stomach. Izzy gasped and the arms dropped to his belly. Hardin grabbed Busy Izzy's arm and jerked him off the bed. He hurled him into a corner of the room and Izzy squatted on the floor, sobbing and moaning softly. Hardin stood over him.

"I don't want to work up a perspiration punching you," Bart said. "I catch cold too easily. I'll have to use the boot if you don't talk."

Bart drew back his leg.

Izzy cried, "For God's sake, don't! I'll talk. It was Selig. . . ."

Bart waited as Izzy fought for breath.

"Selig gave me a grand," said Izzy. "He was going to give me four more when it was over. I was supposed to get the rest tonight. I thought you was the guy who was bringing it when you knocked. They wanted me to lie low here until the beef was chilled."

"Selig paid you to testify against Joe the Whistler?" Hardin asked.

Izzy pressed his hands against his belly. He began to sob helplessly.

"Don't make me, Hardin! Please don't make me! They'll kill me, you know that."

Bart drew back the foot. "It's up to you," he said.

"Selig had an angle," Izzy said hurriedly. "He had it figured out. He said whenever a prosecution witness sat on the stand and told a lie and the judge found out that he was lying he dismissed the case. He said it had happened half a dozen times. He said it was better than fixing the jury, even, because you never could tell what a juror would do, even after he took the money. He said Joe the Whistler couldn't ever be tried for killing Breck again if I sat on the stand and told a lie about him."

Izzy began to laugh hysterically. Then he sobbed helplessly. "Jesus," he said. "Oh, Jesus Christ. Are they going to find out I talked, Hardin?"

Hardin shrugged. "I don't know," he answered coldly. "They won't find out from me. I think they wanted you to talk. I don't know why."

Izzy moaned. "They're going to kill me," he said softly. "They're going to drop me in the river."

"Maybe," Hardin said. "But you've got more urgent worries, Izzy. I'm still here. I haven't heard enough. I want to hear lots more."

"There ain't much more," said Izzy. "That's almost all there is."

Hardin nudged the man on the floor with his foot. "Keep talking, Izzy. I want the details. I want it all."

"Selig said he'd fix it so I could beat the rap for lying on the stand. He had me go to Buffo's place on September seventh and pick up Joe the Whistler. Buffo was going to remember it because the seventh was his birthday, but he wasn't going to remember it till later. He was going to have another witness, too, some society guy that's a barfly there. I picked up the Whistler. I took him up to Breck's place. They knew Breck wasn't home. He was out in Hollywood and he wasn't due back until the eighth. The Whistler stayed inside awhile, then he came out and I drove him to his apartment on Park Avenue. That's all there was."

Hardin's foot nudged Izzy again. "Go on," Bart said. "What about the eighth?"

"Selig fixed up a card game. Right in this hotel. He arranged for three of the boys to be here. He framed you into being here, too, because he figured it was your testimony that would do the trick. The judge wouldn't put too much stock in what Sleeth and those others said. You were Selig's trump card, Hardin. Selig told me to barge into the card game at two-thirty and say that I was looking for him. He told me to stay around for half an hour at least. If you hadn't remembered the date, Sleeth or one of the others would have reminded you. But you remembered the date and the time all right because you played a hunch number on the eighth. They didn't have to remind you."

The man on the floor looked up imploringly at Hardin. "What else you want to know?" he asked. "I've told you all there is. I waited for a week or so after the murder, then I went down to the D.A. and I told my story. The cops kept me on ice as a material witness. They had me in a hotel over in Brooklyn, so the boys wouldn't get to me. I had to laugh. Breakfast in bed, steak on the cops every night. Plenty of room-service liquor. And I was getting paid five grand by Selig for taking a vacation."

Hardin said, "Go on, Izzy. I haven't heard enough. I want to know about Benny Merusi. I want to know about the butterfly."

Izzy shook his head. "I don't know. I heard Benny was chilled, that's all. The cops had me when it happened. I heard about the butterfly. It was some kind of joke. There was some kind of picture of a butterfly, I heard. They wanted it. They thought you had it and you wouldn't give it to them. They framed it so the Old Sarge picked up the butterfly somewhere and then they mugged him and took it and that's all I know. Except the vest. Selig had a gag about a vest with butterflies. It was supposed to be a laugh but you got sore and threw coffee in Selig's face and he's out to get you. That's all I know, Hardin. So help me God, that's all I know."

"Who killed Benny?" Bart demanded.

"I don't know, Hardin. I swear to God I don't know. The cops had me when Benny got chilled. How could I know?"

"Why did they want the picture of the butterfly?" Bart asked.

"I don't know, I don't know, I told you that," said Izzy desperately. "It was supposed to be some kind of gag or something. For God's sake, Hardin, don't belt me any more."

Hardin turned his back on Izzy and walked to the door.

"You can get up off the floor, Izzy," he said. "I'm leaving."

Izzy didn't get up.

He sprawled on the floor, his breath coming in gasps. He was sobbing. He said, "Help me, Hardin. Tell me what to do."

Hardin had his hand on the knob. He looked back at Izzy.

"I'd run if I were you," he said. "I'd start running right now, Izzy. I wouldn't even wait to put my shirt on."

Bart left the room, walked down the corridor to the elevator. He rang the bell and waited a long while for the elevator to reach his floor. When he got off the elevator the lobby was still deserted except for the clerk who was sitting beside the switchboard. The clerk plugged into a line.

The phone in the little office rang. There were four men in the office now. Charley had come in to join the others. Joe the Whistler answered the phone, said "Okay." He hung up the phone. "Hardin's come down," he said. "Pick him up again, Charley. Tail him and check in."

Charley nodded. He rose, opened the door a crack and peered out into the lobby. Presently he went out the door.

The man called Boston said, "Do I take over now?"

"No," said Joe the Whistler. "I take over now."

There was a glass of whisky on the desk in front of him. He drank it unhurriedly. He wiped his lips and rose from the chair. He walked out into the lobby, whistling through his teeth as usual.

There were phone booths in the lobby of the hotel. Bart glanced at his watch. It was eighteen minutes to one. There was time to get to Manhattan West before the hour he had given Romano was up. But Romano's nervous stomach might be troubling him. Bart decided to call in. He did not wish to use the phone booths in the lobby. If they wanted him, it would be easier for them in the lobby than on the street. Hardin walked out of the hotel. He saw a bar down the street near Ninth. He went into the bar and called Romano.

"It's over and I'm all right," he said. "I've learned a little, but not enough. I'm coming down."

"Company's always welcome," Romano said. "It gets real

lonesome for a man down here when nobody talks to him."

Hardin found a cab on Ninth Avenue, a downtown street. It was three minutes to one when he went into the old building on Twentieth that was the clearing house for all the crimes of violence on the west side of Manhattan. Charley's cab was right behind him, but Hardin didn't see it.

Hardin mounted the worn stairs to Romano's office.

The lieutenant appeared to be sitting in exactly the same position as before. The little bottle of pills, the thermos jug and a cup with dregs of coffee were on the desk.

The lieutenant said, "Hello, honey boy. How's everything in the world outside? There haven't been any breaks. Not yet."

Bart said, "Izzy talked. It was a frame. But Izzy knows nothing about Benny or about the butterfly."

Hardin told Romano of the events of the last few hours. The lieutenant listened without interrupting once.

When Bart had finished, Romano said, "I don't like it. I don't like Joe the Whistler tipping you off where that creep Izzy was. It makes my big Italian nose smell something."

Bart said, "It doesn't add. Nothing in the whole damned business adds."

"It could add, all right," Romano replied. "Only I don't like what it adds up to."

Romano thought awhile and then he said, "I didn't know just how they worked it, but I figured the Izzy business for just about what Izzy said it was. Selig was using the law to help one of his boys get away with murder. We might use what we know to get the Commissioner to put the heat on the mob, the way I wanted to in the first place. If the D.A. could be convinced that they made a sucker out of all of us, he'd use the heat. The only trouble is they'd think that I was talking throught my hat to save my job. If we take Izzy down to the D.A., I don't think he'd talk. You couldn't belt Izzy around again with the D.A. looking on. I wish to God I wasn't in so bad with everybody. I'd move in right now and pick Izzy up if I wasn't. But if I did, if I had to trump up some charge to hold him, it really would be curtains, the way things are."

"Romano," Bart said, "the butterfly's the answer. For God's sake, can't you try to remember about the butterfly?"

The swarthy detective shoook his head sadly. He wiped perspiration from his face. He said, "I don't even know now if there *is* something to remember. Your mind plays tricks on you sometimes. When you mentioned a butterfly at that museum last night it rang a little bell. But I'm not sure. I thought there'd been a butterfly mixed up in the Breck case somewhere. If there was, it didn't seem important at the time and I've forgotten because so many other things have happened."

"Even if you didn't have much time to question Joe the Whistler, you must have mentioned the butterfly to him," Bart said. "You must have thought it was important. You told Joe the Whistler that Benny had given me the butterfly."

"My memory's not that bad," Romano declared. "I didn't tell the Whistler you had the butterfly. I didn't even get a chance to mention the butterfly to him. Saltus put the handcuffs on me, but quick."

Bart looked at Romano for a long while before he realized the full import of his answer. Finally he said, "But you must see what that means! Joe said you told him I had the butterfly. That's why he came to me to try and buy it. He knew Benny gave me the butterfly. If he didn't get the information from you, he had to have gotten it from Benny! And if he got it from Benny, he got it after Benny saw me. That means Joe learned about the butterfly at the museum last night. It means he was with Benny . It means he killed him!"

Romano said, "I never doubted that he killed him. But you're jumping too fast again. Joe Merusi's lie is enough to convince you and me that he killed his brother. It's not enough to make the D.A. take him in. Not the way things are."

Bart shook his head impatiently. "It's another day, already, Romano," he said. "We've got to make some move. What do we do now?"

Romano said, "I'm still sitting. I guess I'll keep on sittting. I'm getting stupid in my old age. Sitting's the only thing I can think to do."

"Can't you call the D.A. or the Commissioner and tell them what Izzy admitted? Can't you convince them they should take him in, anyway?"

"Not now, I can't," Romano said wearily. "It would be a waste of time after what has happened. I went out on my own last night because I was sore, and I'm paying for it. It would make the D.A. and the Commissioner real mad if we called them up at one o'clock. It might make them even madder than they are already."

The telephone rang.

Romano said, "You got a rabbit foot in your pocket? Rub it, if you have. This could be the break."

He answered the telephone. He grunted and made monosyllablic answers. He took notes on a small piece of paper.

It was impossible to judge from Romano's face whether the news was good or bad, whether it was important or trivial. In any event, it was lengthy.

Bart had stubbed out one cigarette and lighted another before the lieutenant finally hung up.

Even then, he did not speak at once.

He sat staring hard at Bart and his eyes were sad, defeated.

He said at last, "That was the break. But not for us."

He rose from his chair and got the coat and hat Hardin had hung on a clothes tree in the office. He tossed them in Hardin's lap.

"I guess the Commissioner was right, " Romano said. "I guess I'm getting old. When you get old, you don't remember things. I don't remember a damn thing that you just told me, for instance. Not one word. I bet that three minutes after you're out of this office, I'll even have forgot that you were here."

Bart did not answer. He waited for Romano to speak again.

"That was a murder squeal that just came in," the lieutenant said. "It seems somebody murdered Busy Izzy in room 715 of the Mid-City Hotel. It seems there were some marks on Izzy. He'd been cuffed around. But he wasn't beat to death. He had a bullet in him."

Romano paused long enough to take a pill and swallow water.

"A room clerk and a girl who is a hustler saw a fellow who went up to Izzy's room just a little while ago," Romano coninued. "The girl was in the room and she can identify the man. She said he was tall and had a broken nose and wore a trenchcoat and he had on one of those fancy vests. You know anybody around Broadway answers that description? So long, Hardin. Sorry you can't stay."

fourteen

Charley sat in the parked cab watching the police station. When he saw Hardin come out, he looked perplexed. I guess the cops didn't get the news yet, he thought. They let him walk right out. I wonder where the hell he's going now?

Hardin walked toward Eighth Avenue. Charley said to the driver, who had parked the Red Feather cab in the shadows and turned off his lights, "Give him a lead, then pull up to the corner. He's gonna take another cab, I think."

Hardin wondered how long it would take the cops to put a name to the man with a broken nose who wore a fancy vest. Maybe Romano could stall it for an hour or so but not much longer. The fancy vest was a kind of trademark and trademarks are easily recognizable. He had, maybe, an hour before they put the arm on him. It was around one-thirty now. He had an hour to solve the riddle of the butterfly—if he was lucky.

There was one chance, so faint it was hardly a chance at all. The odds, he figured, were about the same as the odds against catching a royal flush in stud. Gamblers had calculated those odds as 649,740 to 1. But he had to take the odds, because there wasn't any other chance at all.

He had intended to have old Jim Lennox check the clips in the paper's morgue to see if there was any reference to a butterfly in the life of Stephanie Breck. Jim hadn't checked the clips because of the pressure of work in filling the gaping columns of the paper. It had seemed such a longshot that it was hardly worth the effort. Now it was the only thing left to do. When a man is desperate enough, even a straw may seem to be a life raft.

Hardin hailed a cab and directed the driver to the *Broadway Times*. He didn't think the cops would seek him there at this time of night. He would at least have time to go through the motions, to make the gesture, however futile it might seem.

140

A police siren shrilled and a prowl car circled around the cab. Hardin averted his head, almost as if it were a reflex action. So I've learned what it feels like to be a fugitive already, he thought. He grinned wryly. He looked through the rear window of the cab. Another cab was back of them. Hardin thought the markings were those of a Red Feather cab. He wondered if Joe the Whistler was having him tailed. It didn't seem to matter very much.

When the cab was half a block from the *Broadway Times* Hardin saw that a cop was standing in front of the old building. The cop just seemed to be idling. He was swinging his nightstick. But Hardin stopped the cab and got out. He paid the driver, moved back into an entranceway and watched the cop across the street. Presently the cop strolled off. When he was out of sight, Hardin crossed the street rapidly and hurried inside the newspaper office. The place was dimly lighted. Hardin halted suddenly and backed against a wall in the cavernous, shadow-haunted city room. He heard a snorting, animal sound in the room. He stood frozen against the wall for a moment, listening. When his eyes became accustomed to the semi-darkness, he grinned. Old Tim Dargan, the watchman, was sound asleep in Pops Taylor's chair at the horseshoe copy desk. He was snoring loudly.

Bart tiptoed by the desk, walked up a long, dark corridor to the morgue where newspaper clippings, reference books, cuts, photographs were filed. He went inside and switched on a light. He left the door open. The morgue was a treasure house of old and dusty memories. Here, in stiff Manila envelopes, filed alphabetically, were the records of men and women who had known brief fame or notoriety on a street called Broadway. Many of them were dead now and most of them were forgotten. They existed only in their little Manila domiciles as words on yellowed, crumbling newsprint. The pace of Broadway is too fast for memories.

One side of the morgue was devoted to filed clippings, another to photographs, mats and cuts. On the wall beside a window was a bookcase that reached almost ceiling-high. It sagged from an overload of reference books, encyclopedias, dictionaries, atlases, thesauruses, almanacs and theatrical yearbooks. A heavy truck passed in the street and the flimsy bookcase with its heavy freight shook and trembled. Bart made a mental note that the shelves should be attached to the wall by angle irons. He did not want this load of tomes crashing down on the red head of Orville Cartwright, the copy boy and custodian of the morgue. Hardin shook his head. It was hard to realize he might not be there to make such small arrangements.

Bart took off his coat and began to thumb through envelopes until he found the clippings on Stephanie Breck. Her publicity agents had been extremely active. There were three envelopes and all of them were stuffed to the bursting point.

He sat down at Orville's desk and shook out the contents of one of the envelopes. He switched on a gooseneck lamp, adjusted it and began to read.

Stephanie's real name was Josie Casey, he learned. Her Hollywood name had been Stephanie Karel. There were many photographs with the stories. During her early career, most of the photographs showed Stephanie in a bathing suit or rompers or costumes equally adapted to showing off her anatomical assets, which were considerable. Then, when she had become a star, she was pictured in evening gowns and sports costumes with sweaters that were almost as revealing. Finally, when she had attained the distinction of becoming Mrs. Breck, the photographs were more decorous, mostly what photographers call head-shots. But the photographers still included as much of Stephanie's bosom as they could.

The stories were many and varied. There were the outright, gushing, hyped-up studio press releases, the hints that she was descended from an old and noble Hungarian family, the usual build-up about her dining out with male stars of the time. Then there were the reviews of her pictures and all of them said that Stephanie was a very nice thing for any man to look at, but couldn't act a lick. Finally, in this stage of her career, there was the gossip. Some of it bordered on libel and all of it indicated that Stephanie was a tramp.

The tone of the stories changed suddenly after Stephanie's marriage to the highly respected Jason Breck. At this point she was mentioned mainly in the society columns that Mrs. Washburn wrote, in connection with benefit performances she sponsored or balls for the Actors' Fund.

Bart read through the clippings in the first envelope. The morgue was silent except for the occasional hum of the city outside. Twenty minutes had already passed. He did not have much more time. And he had found no butterfly.

The second envelope was just as unrewarding and nearly three-quarters of an hour had gone by before he finished it.

Hardin wondered how long it would take the cops to come to the office to seek him out, how long the strategems of Romano might hold them off. His eyes were becoming bleary from reading the columns of eight-point type set only fourteen picas wide. He put the second envelope away and attacked the third and final one. This, he thought, is really the last chance.

Hardin was half through the last envelope of clippings when his body suddenly stiffened and his eyes stared unbelievingly.

He saw the butterfly at last.

The butterfly was there, right before his eyes.

Ironically, the story that accompanied the photo of the butterfly had been written by Mrs. Washburn. He had asked Mrs. Washburn about the butterfly only a few hours before. Like Romano, she had forgotten. That was understandable. The story had been written four years ago.

Hardin read the story.

> . . . and her collection of antique jewelry, all of which once bedecked the throats and heads and arms and necks of some of history's most famous women, is simply fabulous and beyond price. At the Actors' Fund Ball last evening, Stephanie wore the famous Empress Josephine tiara of diamonds and sapphires and the Pompadour ear-drops that eighteenth-century goldsmiths fashioned cunningly in the shape of tiny lyres with perfectly matched pearls.
>
> The most unusual item in Stephanie's collection, however, is a necklace she never wears. It is far too uncomfortable on her pretty neck, she says. This is the extraordinary Butterfly Necklace, a veritable rainbow array of rubies, emeralds, sapphires, topazes and other precious and semi-precious stones fashioned in the shape of a butterfly. The butterfly is two inches high and twice as wide and is attached to a collar of seed pearls that covers almost the entire neck. "The tips of the wings stick in my chin," Stephanie says. "I can't possibly wear it, but it's very beautiful." The Butterfly Necklace was designed especially for Louise of Austria, one of the great beauties of the Napoleonic era. The poor lady had an unsightly goiter, and being as vain as most pretty ladies, she always attempted to conceal the defect. . . .

Bart rose from the chair and crossed to the wall where photographs were filed. The reproduction of the Butterfly

Necklace was dim and grainy, but if there had been a cut, there had to be an original photograph, too. Hardin found the photograph after a search that lasted for several minutes. He sat down again and put the glossy print on the desk in front of him. The gooseneck lamp shed harsh, bright light on the butterfly.

There wasn't any doubt about it.

This was the butterfly that Benny Merusi had painted, the butterfly that had cost Benny his life.

The Butterfly Necklace had a star-shaped design in its middle, just the way that Benny's own butterfly had been marked.

It was clear enough to Hardin now. He knew why the Whistler's brother had been murdered and he knew how he had died.

The answer had not only been locked in Romano's mind and lost in Mrs. Washburn's wandering memory. It had been right there within easy reach of Hardin all the time, right in his own office.

Only he hadn't bothered to reach.

It was all so ridiculously obvious now.

Joe the Whistler had taken the paste jewels after he killed Breck in order to make the crime appear to be a burglary just in case something should go wrong with his perjured witness, Izzy. The jewels had made a bulky parcel, not too easy to dispose of. The Whistler had given the package to his brother Benny to keep, to hide, knowing Benny could be completely trusted. But Benny had been like a child in many ways. He had had a child's curiosity. While the Whistler was in jail awaiting trial, Benny had peeped into the package his brother left with him. He had been fascinated by the shiny, brightly colored butterfly and he had painted it.

Bart remembered how he had thought, even upon a cursory examination, that Benny's butterfly painting had glowed like stained glass. That should have been the tipoff. Benny's painting had glowed because Benny was painting jewels.

Hardin remembered now, too, the strange concern that Stephanie had shown when she found him examining the miniature of a historic personage called Louise of Austria. He had thought nothing of it at the time, however, had not connected the miniature of the woman who wore a wispy, blowing scarf with the butterfly a mentally retarded youth had painted.

When Joe the Whistler had been released, Benny had told

him proudly about painting the butterfly. The Whistler had been furious, of course, and had demanded Benny's painting to destroy it. Benny had managed to stall his brother somehow because he did not wish to destroy the work he considered his masterpiece. He had probably agreed to meet his brother at the museum that evening and give him the painting. Instead he had given it to Bart.

The Whistler had doubtless obtained the paste jewels and gotten rid of them as soon as he was released. But he knew that if Benny's painting was compared to the real Butterfly Necklace that still reposed in a bank vault, it could be established easily that each colored stone was in the exact place it was supposed to be, that Benny had seen the missing paste replica and had painted it. The police would know immediately that Joe the Whistler must have had the necklace and that meant that he must have murdered Breck. They could not try Joe again for Breck's murder. But the Whistler was fully aware of what almost always happened when a hoodlum beat a rap through some legal trickery. The police bore down on him and hounded him and sometimes made him so hot the mob found it necessary to liquidate him. It had happened before. And the police did not stop there. They hounded the entire Syndicate and all its enterprises, and the profits were cut on nearly every operation of the mob, for a time, at least. Joe the Whistler would not be popular with Selig or with the big boss, Lenny Fassio, if that happened.

The Whistler had met Benny at the museum the night before. He had dominated his younger brother for many years and it had not been hard for him to make Benny confess that he had given the painting of the butterfly to Hardin. Joe had been enraged and had struck his brother, probably with a blackjack he carried in his pocket, and Benny had died.

The Whistler had to get the painting. Even if Bart had seen it, it did not matter too much. Probably he had not connected it with the Butterfly Necklace. Benny had painted only the butterfly. He had not painted the seed-pearl collar. But so long as the painting itself existed, the Whistler was in danger. Someone might make the connection and they might compare the picture, stone by stone, with the original in the bank vault.

The Whistler had fled to Stephanie's house, just a few blocks away, after Benny's murder. He and Stephanie had made it appear they had been in an intimate situation for some time before the arrival of the police.

Romano had doubtless seen a description of the butterfly in the list of property missing from the Breck house. That was what had been in his mind. But it had not seemed important at the time and Romano had forgotten it.

When Romano was forced to release the Whistler, Joe had needed help in obtaining the butterfly. He had gone to Selig and the great butterfly chase of Broadway had begun. Finally, the mob had obtained the painting by having someone call the Old Sarge and pretend that he was Lennox, Hardin's "secretary." They knew Marty Land would accept the Old Sarge as Hardin's emissary without question. When the Old Sarge had the painting, they simply mugged him, took it, and destroyed it.

It was typical of the mobster mind that they could not help gloating when they had achieved their aim and considered Hardin and Romano helpless. That accounted for Selig's crude jest with the embroidered vest.

Hardin sat staring at the photograph of the Butterfly Necklace for several minutes, shaking his head.

He was staring at the butterfly when he heard a small sound directly behind him.

Someone was whistling very softly through his teeth.

fifteen

Hardin turned and faced Joe the Whistler.

The Whistler had a gun in his hand.

The gun was pointing at Hardin.

The Whistler said, "So now you know."

Hardin said, "Yes, I know."

The Whistler looked sad. He said, "That's too bad, Hardin. I didn't come here to kill you. I told you that I like you. I like you, but I've got to kill you just the same. I came here to help you out because you're in a jam. The cops want you for chilling Izzy. I figured you might be broke since you were chump enough to give the ten gees to Marty Land. I figured you might need some money so you could run. I was going to give you some money. Not ten grand again, but enough to run a good, long way. I figured I owed it to you. You saved my life, even if you didn't mean to."

The Whistler sighed. "I guess it's better this way, though," he said. "It ties it all up. The gun can't be traced. It's the gun that killed Izzy a little while ago. It's the gun I'm going to kill you with now, Hardin. I'll put it up close when I squeeze the trigger, so there'll be powder burns. Then I'll wipe it off and I'll put it in your hand. The cops will figure you chilled Izzy and did the Dutch act. It'll tie it up real nice for them."

The Whistler chuckled. "I always like to help the cops when it's convenient," he said.

Hardin's eyes moved briefly toward the door. He shook his head almost imperceptibly. He said, "It should be easy enough to kill me, Whistler, you've had a lot of practice lately. You killed Breck and you killed Benny."

"Yes, I killed Breck," the Whistler said. "I had to kill poor Benny, too. I didn't want to kill him. I loved Benny, Hardin.

147

I really did. But I had to kill him just the same. I do what I've got to do."

The Whistler grinned. "You skipped one, Hardin," he said. "You're going to be the fourth. I killed Izzy, too. You were a real chump, walking into that one, Hardin. You play it rough, but you're kind of stupid, chum. The room clerk saw you at the hotel. The broad saw you, too. They can identify you. Five minutes after you'd gone, I put a bullet in Izzy's head. We'd have had to do it sooner or later anyway. You can't trust Izzy's type. I could have let Boston or Charley do it, but I wanted to be sure it was done right."

The Whistler looked down curiously at Hardin. "Why does your head keep shaking, chum?" he asked. "You getting kind of nervous? Well, I won't make you wait. This is it."

He put the gun against Hardin's temple.

There was a sudden yell and the Whistler turned.

Tim Dargan, the old watchman who had been standing at the door for fully sixty seconds with a look of paralyzed shock on his face, was hurtling toward the Whistler. His old body crashed into the man with the gun. The gun went off, but the shot went wild and the Whistler was slammed to the floor.

Bart sprang from the chair. The gun slithered across the floor, out of reach.

Tim Dargan lay on the floor. He had banged his head against the desk in diving at the Whistler.

The Whistler scrambled to his fee. He smashed his fist into Hardin's jaw and Bart staggered back against a wall. The Whistler was on him at once, raining punches. "Okay, okay," he was gasping. "I do it with my hands." He hit Bart flush on the chin and Hardin felt his knees go weak. The Whistler poised, measured, drew back his fist. "I'm on my feet, Hardin," he said. "This time I ain't sitting down."

Hardin brought up a hard left. It grazed the chin and destroyed the force of the Whistler's punch. The Whistler retreated a step and Bart, still dazed, shaking his befuddled head, went after him. He sank one to the belly. The Whistler sent in two that were hard and that hurt. Hardin pounded through the Whistler's guard with a left, crossed with the right.

The Whistler staggered back. His heavy body crashed into the rickety bookcase. The bookcase teetered for a second, then it plunged downward, spewing heavy reference books down on the Whistler.

The Whistler was lying on his stomach and he was very still.

A small mountain of heavy books blanketed the Whistler.

Bart was swaying on his feet. He raised a hand to his battered chin. His whole jaw felt numb. A thin trickle of blood was drooling from his mouth.

Moving very slowly and very carefully, he found the gun. He leaned down to pick it up. A fit of dizziness surged over him and he had to support himself against a filing cabinet.

With the gun in his hand, he staggered over and bent down at the side of old Tim Dargan. Tim's eyes fluttered open. He said, "I—I must have hit my head. Are you all right?"

"I'm fine," Bart answered. He spit out blood. "You saved my life, Tim."

The old man smiled and raised himself to a sitting position. "You saved my wife's life once, Mr. Bart," he answered.

Tim looked at the recumbent body of the Whistler. "Is he dead?" he asked.

"I'll see," Bart replied.

He bent down beside the Whistler. He pushed a mound of books off the Whistler's body.

"He's breathing," Bart told Tim. "He's just knocked out."

Old Tim was sitting in a chair now, his hand pressed against the lump on his forehead. "I heard him," he said. "I heard him say he'd killed three men."

Hardin picked up the telephone.

He called Romano.

It took twelve minutes exactly for Romano and a large young detective named Grierson and the ambulance men to arrive.

They found Bart with a gun in his hand and a sodden handkerchief pressed against his bleeding mouth. Old Tim had taken a lump of ice from a water-cooler and was holding it against his head.

Joe the Whistler still slept peacefully on the floor among the literary shambles.

Romano looked down at the Whistler and the pile of heavy books that almost covered him.

"Joe the Whistler looks real educated, don't he?" Romano said.

Hardin told Romano about the butterfly. He told him that Tim Dargan had heard the Whistler confess three murders and had seen him attempt another one.

"This time I can take him in," Romano said. "Only we've got to take him on a stretcher."

"Go down to City Hospital with 'em," Romano said to the young detective. "Tell 'em there's a hold on the Whistler. Tell 'em it's a private room in the locked ward and a cop sitting outside the door."

When they had carried the Whistler out, Hardin said, "You can laugh in the Commissioner's face this afternoon, Romano. You'll be right back near the top of the Captain's List again."

"Yeah," Romano replied with his usual pessimism. "I'll probably be right near the top for years and years and never make it. They'll keep putting young cops up over me. The kind that have got a college education."

Hardin glanced at his watch. "There's still time for a drink at the Sligo Slasher's," he declared. "Let's go out and celebrate."

Romano shook his head, "I'm on the wagon," he said. "My nervous duodenal has been acting up again."

A smile flickered on the lieutenant's swarthy face.

"I've got butterflies in my stomach," Romano said.